NIGHT DRIFTER

AN EDWARD MENDEZ, P. I. THRILLER

BOOK 2

Gerard Denza

Night Drifter:
An Edward Mendez, P.I. Thriller
Book II

Copyright 2019 Gerard Denza

All rights reserved.
ISBN: 978-1-7328653-1-0

Cover art: Book Covers Art

www.gerarddenza.com

Also available digitally.

By the same author:

-ICARUS: THE COLLECTED PLAYS

-RAMSAY: DEALER OF DEATH

-THE TIME DECEIVER:
AN EDWARD MENDEZ, P. I. THRILLER, BOOK I

-NIGHT DRIFTER:
AN EDWARD MENDEZ, P. I. THRILLER, BOOK II

To
Phil Strumolo

MAIN CHARACTERS

Edward Mendez - a private investigator with a troubled and hidden past who has only days to save the world and learn about his own dark history.

Werner Hoffman, Jr. - a young man who wants Edward to find an ancient artifact that may save the world or destroy it.

Yolanda Estravades - a beautiful figure skater who must chose between her career and helping her boyfriend save the world.

Lt. William Donovan - a police detective on a personal vendetta who suspects Edward and Yolanda of having committed murder.

Dolores Sarney - a young woman who was murdered by demons.

Susan Broder - Marlena Lake's daughter who will have to match her wits with a top scientist.

A middle-aged woman - a ruthless murderer who may not be human.

Male pursuer - a ruthless murderer who may not be human.

Marlena Lake - a resourceful and treacherous woman who knows more about the earths's predicament than she's telling.

Fred - a savvy New York City cabbie.

Werner Hoffman, Sr. - an ex-Nazi who regrets his past mistakes.

Nella Mendez - Edward's sister and a dabbler in the occult sciences. She has many secrets from her younger brother.

Nathalie Montaigne - an ex-Nazi who is a friend of the Hoffmans and now finds herself in America.

Isabelle Mendez - Edward's reclusive mother who was once married to the leader of a powerful occult group, a man she still fears.

Wulf Holderman - a book shop owner, thief, and Nazi.

Professor Charles Lange - an astronomer and occultist who may also be a traitor to humanity.

Mary Riley - Professor Lange's able assistant who is most observant.

Victoria Mendez-Gonzalez - Edward's beautiful and naive sister.

Ramon Gonzalez - Victoria's murdered husband.

Angel Ulysses Correa - a young man and bodybuilder who has been turned into a monster. He's hunting for his first victim and isn't too choosey about who he selects.

Dottie Mendez - Edward's sister who is a sports enthusiast and cat lover. Her next door neighbor just happens to be inhuman.

Sgt. Tom Rayno - Lt. Donovan's young assistant who doesn't believe in magic.

Catrina Mendez - an acerbic and self-centered woman with no imagination. She has lived in fear of someone all her life.

Gabriel Broder - Marlena Lake's son who never returned from Egypt.

Stripes - a tabby cat who lives in the neighborhood candy store.

Mrs. Jack - a candy store owner who is down on her luck.

Table of Contents

PROLOGUE

...and the light of the world was extinguished. The earth became a night drifter in the darkness of space.

PART I

BLACK-OUT
December 12, 1947

CHAPTER ONE

EDWARD MENDEZ had been back in New York City
for eight months: a private investigator working out of
a downtown office in Manhattan on the corner of John
St. and Broadway. His office was in the front of an old
sandstone building with a clear view of pedestrian and
vehicular traffic. The P. I. enjoyed the noise and the
voices of the city…his city. He got a kick out of listening
to people's conversations on the street and in the subway. You never knew what you might overhear.

Lower Manhattan was a part of town that Edward
loved and knew like the back of his hand: every ham-
burger joint, greasy spoon, and two-bit candy store
and…a lot of nightclubs. He'd even been to the Stock
Exchange a few times on client business and for his own
rare investments. And, every once in a while, he'd head
into his favorite haberdashers on Gold St. and pick up
an inexpensive suit and a couple of pairs of argyle socks.

Back in April, Edward had suffered a curious form of amnesia: his past had been a complete blank slate. For several weeks, he couldn't even recall his own name. He'd since recovered his memory, except for the few hours that had led up to his illness. Those few hours remained hidden and for some reason, he thought that that brief lapse in memory was vital; but, vital to what and to whom? He didn't have a clue. Where had he been before he'd found himself lying on that slab of ice in the skating rink up in midtown? He couldn't remember…it just wouldn't come and he thought about it a lot. What had he done earlier on that particular day?

-The hell with it for now. I'm not gonna' dwell on it. What's the damned use? Something or someone is bound to trigger that lapse in time.

At this moment, on a cold but sunny and pleasant Sunday afternoon in December, he was sitting at his desk and playing "rocket ship" with his fountain pen. He was bored. The downtown area of Manhattan was like a graveyard on the weekend: a canyon of near empty skyscrapers. He was thinking about that pretty, blonde girl he'd been flirting with on his way to work. He'd noticed her standing near the subway car doors looking sexy and bored. Was she on her way to work on a Sunday? Well, why not? He was. Maybe, she had an unorthodox job like his. She had a lovely, slim figure and the black dress with the "spaghetti" straps that she'd been wearing had accentuated every sensual curve of her magnificent body. The black high-heels were the finishing touch. Oh, yes.

But, why was she standing up and pretending not to notice him? There were plenty of empty seats in the car; although he would have gladly offered her his own. She probably had a date waiting for her and as well she should. It would be a crime if that weren't the case. And, was this chick smelling his new after shave cologne: Williams After Shave? His current girlfriend, Yolanda, had picked it out especially for him. Yes. She was turning him into a well-groomed man about town. Edward's sisters had noticed the subtle changes in their brother…a woman's influence, to be sure.

Putting that memory to the back of his mind, for the moment, he looked at the two books that he'd purchased from the Anne St. book shop just a few blocks away: an American Heritage dictionary and a Thesaurus. He smiled as he flipped through the pages of the dictionary. He never had one of his own and his sister, Nella, said that every self-respecting gentleman should.

The word "parallel" caught his attention: "extending in the same direction and at the same distance apart so as to never meet."

-Hmm. I wonder if this definition applies to people, too? I'd make bet that it does. Walking in the same direction and never to meet. How many people have I never met? How many times have I walked alongside of someone without even noticing her…except, of course, if she were good looking?

Edward straightened his tie and put on his suit jacket. It was chilly in his office despite the sun's rays filtering in. He could see the tiny dust particles floating in the air and he remembered that as a little boy, he would try to catch them in the palm of his hand. How long ago that moment seemed. How different his world had been back then.

The phone on his desk rang and this got Edward out of his reverie. He looked at his wristwatch: 3:40. Who would be calling him on a late Sunday afternoon? Hopefully, it was a client, but it was more likely to be Yolanda and this brought a smile to his handsome face. Yolanda was even more beautiful than that blonde chick he'd been eyeing on the subway. She was a Latin beauty who knew every trick and maneuver in bed and out. He was already semi-erect.

As he was about to pick up the phone's receiver the world went dark for a second. Had a biplane or zeppelin passed in front of the sun?

-What was that? Did the lights blink out or something?

The moment passed and the phone kept ringing. This time, the P. I. picked up the receiver.

-Edward Mendez.

-Mr. Mendez? My name is Werner Hoffman. You don't know me, but I know of you as a a private investigator.

-It's what I do, Mr. Hoffman. How can I help you?

-I must see you immediately. I'm across the street calling from the A.T.&T. building in the lobby. I wanted to make certain that you were in your office.

-Come on up, Mr. Hoffman. My office is on the tenth floor. Make a right when you step out of the elevator. I'll be waiting for you. The building is open.

-Yes. I know.

-It's almost four o'clock. I can give you about an hour, if you like. The building closes at five, and I don't plan on staying much beyond that.

-I know.

-You're pretty well informed. I'll be expecting you.

Edward put the receiver down.

And, so did Werner Hoffman, Jr. He placed the phone back in its cradle, opened the accordion door and stepped out of the booth. His purpose to America would now begin. He would carry out his father's instructions…orders. The young man didn't like what he was about to undertake, but he had little choice in the matter. HIs boat had arrived from Germany only two days ago and he was still fatigued from the rough crossing. No matter. Rest was no longer a luxury he could afford. He'd traveled first class and he was now housed in an upscale Manhattan apartment. All had been arranged. He was a puppet; a wealthy puppet, but certainly he was not in control of his destiny. This thought brought a wry smile to his pale face.

-Was any man in control of his destiny? Was a man's path in life decided for him at birth? Were all of a man's choices pre-ordained by some deity? If that were true, how pointless this made life.

He stopped his petty attempt at philosophy.

Hoffman's money was founded in gold: blood soaked gold from the many innocent and not-so-innocent corpses that lay strewn across Europe and Asia. He knew this and it did burden his conscience which was not such a good thing for an ex-Nazi to have because it made life quite painful.

Werner Hoffman stepped outside on to the sidewalk and looked up at the sky; not a cloud in the heavens. He crossed the street and headed toward Edward Mendez's building. How many more will have to die? A good question that could only be answered by the dictates of expediency.

In another moment, Hoffman was waiting for the elevator that would take him to the top floor and the P. I.'s office. He must stay calm and make his case clearly and urgently. Difficult. There was much hidden history to the demands that he would make on the private investigator and much of that history must remain hidden.

The elevator arrived and he got in. Now, why was this elevator operator staring at him? He could at least be discreet about his curiosity: an ill-mannered young man.

-Tenth floor, please.

-Sure.

The vertical ride was quick.

-Tenth floor.

-Thank you.

-Where you headed for? Mendez's office?

-Please, mind your own business. Good day.

-Werner Hoffman. Now, where the hell have I heard that name before? Was it after I came back from Egypt with Yolanda or- No! No. Not *after*, it was right before we left. I came back to check out this office.

Edward slammed down his fist on to the green ink blotter.

-The file on W.W. II and those photos…there were names on the back of one of them. I'd almost forgotten.

The P. I. turned the swivel chair around to face the dove grey filing cabinet. Bending over, he pulled out the bottom draw and took out the manilla folder marked "W.W. II Artifacts." He placed it on his desk and opened it. Inside were photos of an atomic bomb explosion, but for now he wasn't interested in the photos. He flipped them over. On the back of one was a list of names. He read one of them out loud.

-Werner Hoffman: two Werner Hoffmans as a matter of fact: a father and son. It'll be nice to put a face to at least one of the names. Come to think of it, I don't remember having written those names down. Then, maybe, just maybe, I was in my office before I blacked out back in April. But, how did I get from here to Yolanda's skating rink?

The private investigator heard the elevator door slide open, but he couldn't make out the figure who was walking toward his office because of the frosted glass. The figure knocked on the door.

-He's a polite bastard, I'll say that much for him. Come in, Mr. Hoffman.

The door opened and the young man walked in. He was thin and stood about five feet and a half. His manner was almost self-effacing, but he had an air of the aristocrat about him.

Edward stood up and extended his hand to the young man.

-Mr. Hoffman? Edward Mendez. Please, sit down. Make yourself comfortable. There's a coat hanger right behind you.

-Thank you. I hope that I haven't come at a bad time.

-You haven't. Cigarette?

-No. Thank you.

-Do you mind if I smoke?

-Not at all.

Edward took out a cigarette and lit up.

-My girlfriend got me started on a new brand: Pall Mall. They're not too bad; but, I think I'll be sticking with my old brand: Lucky Strike.

He closed the file that he'd just been looking at. He didn't want his new client to see it. He had his reasons Mr. Hoffman, what can I do for you?

-I need your help in locating the Spear of Longinus. It's an ancient artifact and it is priceless.

Edward smiled and lit his cigarette.

-You get straight to the point. I usually locate people, not antiques.

-Are you turning me down, Mr. Mendez? Please don't. I am desperate. And, I am wealthy. You'll be well paid for your efforts.

-I'm not turning you down. And, I'm glad you're well fixed.

Werner Hoffman looked past Edward to peer out the window.

-It's getting dark outside…almost too dark for this time of day.

-Come, again?

Edward turned his chair around to face the window.

-It's December and the days are getting shorter. I think we're just about headed for the shortest one of them all: the winter solstice. And, it's also getting closer to my favorite holiday: Christmas. Do you celebrate Christmas, Mr. Hoffman?

-Yes. I've noticed all the decorations around Herald Square and even in this downtown area.

Edward turned back to face his client.

-Mr. Hoffman? Werner? You're sweating and it's not exactly warm in here. What's up, pal?

-Nothing.

-You sweat over nothing? I think you're holding out on me. And, that's not a good way to start a professional relationship.

-Mr. Mendez, I fear that I'm wasting your time. It's late. Perhaps, I should come back another day.

-No. Don't leave. I want to help you if I can. Try and relax. Your case kind of interests me.

-On second thought, may I have a cigarette? I need one.

-Now, you're talking. Light?

He flipped Hoffman a cigarette.

On the upper east side of Manhattan, in a brownstone townhouse, Yolanda Estravades was having a hard time of it. She was sitting in Marlena Lake's living room and with her was a police detective. The mistress of the house had made herself scarce because policemen of any rank made her nervous.

Yolanda looked about the dark room. How like Marlena to absent herself and leave Yolanda to take the heat. And, where was Marlena's bookworm daughter, Susan? Probably at the main branch of the public library with her nose buried in some book.

Trouble always seemed to follow Yolanda and the young woman knew why. She didn't try to fool herself. Her tastes and aspirations in life were expensive and dangerous in that respective order. She wanted to be the next Olympic gold medalist figure skater and this took dedication, training, and money to afford the best coach, the costumes, and choreographer.

Her boyfriend could not afford to finance her ice skating career and this had forced Yolanda into a making a difficult decision. She'd mended fences with her estranged family and they had graciously consented to help the ambitious figure skater out as much as they could. She was properly grateful.

She stole a glance at the detective. She didn't like him at all. He was handsome in a ruddy, healthy sort of way, but he was definitely not Yolanda's type. No. Edward Mendez was her kind of man: suave and with just a touch of the rough that she liked.

Her thoughts were interrupted.

-Miss Estravades?

-Yes? I'm sorry. I was distracted. There was something outside…a shadow crossing in front of the sun. Would you like me to turn on more lights? It's so dark in here. Marlena prefers the darkness, but I don't.

-If you wouldn't mind. I'd like to see what I'm jotting down.

-Of course not.

Yolanda got up and went over to the the light switch near the doorway. She flipped the switch.

-Better for you, detective? Now, you can see if I'm lying or not and you'll be able to read your notes.

Lt. Donovan leaned back in his char. He was a man who appreciated a good looking woman. And, he damn well knew that Yolanda Estravades fell full throttle into that category. The young woman's slim figure was complimented by her perfect posture and bearing. Her clothes were simple, but clearly of high quality: the dark grey skirt that fell just below the knees, the tailored white blouse and, of course, black high heels for those gorgeous legs. It was hard for the lieutenant not to be distracted, but he somehow managed.

-Let's continue, Miss Estravades.

-I don't mean to be sarcastic, but I don't know what else to tell you, Det. Donovan.

-Lieutenant Donovan. You were friends with Dolores Sarney, weren't you?

-Yes. But, I don't see what that has to do with anything. We were best friends, if you want to know.

-You were the last person to see her alive.

-How do you know that? I don't know it.

-She was last seen in your company at your ice skating rink on 31st St. and 10th Ave.

-What are you trying to say? Are you accusing me of murdering her? I didn't. I was training and Dolores was keeping me company. She often did that. We did lots of things together. She had no family and didn't know that many people.

-Did Miss Sarney leave the ice rink with you?

-No. She got bored and left on her own. It can be very boring to watch someone practice figure eights and straight lines on the ice. I didn't mind.

-She left you alone? That doesn't make sense.

-She knew that my boyfriend was coming to pick me up. I wouldn't be alone for long.

-Did he?

-Yes. He did.

-What's your boyfriend's name?

-HIs name is Edward Mendez. He's a private investigator. Maybe, you know him.

He ignored the question.

-Didn't you and Mr. Mendez take a sudden trip to Germany on that same night?

-We also visited Egypt. And, then, we came back. We've nothing to hide.

-You took a trip to Germany on the same night that your girlfriend was murdered. Your girlfriend, Miss Estravades…the one we fished out of the East River not too long ago.

-If we fled the country, would we have been so foolish as to come back?

-Criminals aren't particularly smart, Miss Estravades.

-I'm no criminal. And, Dolores hasn't been seen for months. How did you know that it was she? Did she tell you? I don't think so.

-We have our methods. It helped that she had I.D. on her. The person or persons who dumped her body in the river were pretty careless. Miss Estravades, your best friend had been slaughtered like a stuck pig.

Susan Broder was getting ready to leave the main branch of the public library at 42nd St. Her mother had sent her on a research trip that had something to do with the sun and its position in the solar system. The young woman knew her mother all too well. When her mother was good and ready, she'd tell her daughter what her reasons were because Marlena Lake had a reason for everything that she did.

Susan had wanted to go to college, but her mother convinced her that this would be a waste of time. The philosophy of Kant had infected the university teaching curriculum. Apart from that, the education that a university offered was incomplete, at best: the subjects were mundane and offered little challenge to the superior mind.

Susan checked out her books at the main desk and put them in her briefcase. She turned to leave, but stopped to admire the architecture of this magnificent building in the heart of mid-town Manhattan: the broad marble stairwells and the arched windows that were nearly two stories tall. After a few moments, she started walking toward the exit and for just a moment, she thought the lights had blinked out.

-What in the world was that?

-Did you notice it, too, dear? It was weird, don't you think?

A plump, middle-aged woman was standing next to Susan.

-I guess the lights in the building flickered off for a moment. I'm sure it's nothing to worry about.

-But, it wasn't the library lights. It was...well, I can't explain it. It seemed to come from the outside.

Susan couldn't explain it either and it bothered her. She looked about the vast hallway and everything was functioning as it should. At the far end of the hallway, a man caught her attention. He was staring at her. He was leaning against the far wall with his hands in his coat pockets. He was hatless. His dark hair was short and disheveled. HIs face was as pale as chalk and his eyes never left Susan's.

-You'll have to excuse me, but I must run.

-No time for a cup of coffee, dear? There's a restaurant right across the street. We can talk about the books we've just checked out.

Susan acquiesced out of politeness and curiosity. There was something distinctly odd about this woman. As they left the main hall, she glanced back at the man who she thought had been staring at her. He was still standing there, stock still and watching her every move.

Susan and her new acquaintance made themselves as comfortable as they could on the stools that were not meant to be too comfortable for patrons. They ordered their coffees amidst the hubbub of the crowd and the waitresses taking orders. The place was well lit but had an almost intimate quality thanks to the overcrowd.

-What's your name, dear?

-Susan Broder

-Yes. What books have you taken out, dear?

-Nothing of great import, really. Books on astronomy and physics.

-How impressive. You look like the studious type, I daresay. Do you live here in the city.

-Yes…

-Where?

Susan dodged the question.

-This coffee is quite good, don't you think?

-Do you live nearby? Within walking distance, I mean? We could share a cab.

-I'm afraid I don't take cabs.

That was a lie. Taking cabs was a luxury that Susan always allowed herself.

-They're much better than the subway. I hate the crowds and noisy underground and the wretched lighting. Which train do you take, Susan?

This woman was insufferable. Who in heaven's name was she? And, her movements were not those of an overweight or middle-aged person either. No. They were the movements and reactions of a much younger woman And, her face was so heavily powdered and rouged…almost like a mask.

Susan thought it was time to make her excuses and leave. It was nearly four oclock, anyway, and time to get home. She put down enough change on the counter to cover the cost of both coffees.

-Leaving, dear?

-I must. Nice talking to you. I didn't catch your name.

-I'll walk to the corner with you.

Was there no getting rid of her?

As Susan stood up to leave, she saw that same man from the library staring into the coffee shop. And, this time, he wasn't looking at her. He and this dreadful woman were looking at each other.

CHAPTER TWO

THE AIR between the P. I. and his new client was filled with drifting cigarette smoke.

-Okay, Mr. Hoffman, give, and don't spare the details. I love 'em.

Werner Hoffman, Jr. took a deep breath. Was Edward's new client annoyed? Too bad.

-I was a young boy of seven when I was taken from my adoptive parents. On that day, they were killed and my true father took me off to Germany to be educated and raised.

Edward was almost impressed.

-You really know how to compress a story into a sentence or two. Were your American parents killed or murdered? There is a difference.

-Eliminated, Mr. Mendez, would be the more accurate term.

-Who did the eliminating? Do you know?

-By supernatural forces, I daresay. I don't mean to sound vague, but it's the best answer that I can give you. Do you believe me?

Edward's smile was broad and genuine.

-Believe it or not, I do. I'm not too unfamiliar with the supernatural…not by a long shot. Now, Mr. Hoffman, who did this eliminating and why?

-I don't know who, but I do know the why.

-I'm listening.

-May I trouble you for another cigarette?

-Sure.

Edward reached into his jacket pocket and took out the pack of Lucky Strike. He handed the pack to his new client.

-Help yourself. Light? This is my brand of cigarette.

-Thank you.

-Now, tell me the why.

-I was to be brought back to Germany to find the Spear of Longinus.

-You mentioned that before. What exactly is that? And, it wasn't in Germany so you came back to America?

The private investigator tried not to grin. He knew that his "friend" Marlena Lake would be all too familiar with any and every supernatural article that ever existed.

-You're grinning, Mr. Mendez. May I ask why? Do I amuse you?

-Not at you, pal. I was thinking about someone else who's also a friend to the supernatural. Now, about the spear?

-It's not easy to put this into mundane words.

-Give it a try. Is it a weapon or a device of sorts? Have you found it and lost it? Was it stolen? And, is it worth anything in, say, monetary terms?

-No, Mr. Mendez, I have never laid eyes on it. And, it is *you* who will find it for me. And, as to its value? It's worth would go beyond any price that could be named.

-I'll make bet that some *could* name a price.

-No doubt.

-I'll need a few clues, if you'll pardon the expression. But, hold off on the spear for just a few seconds. For some reason and, I'm not too sure why, the killing of your adoptive parents interests me.

-It should. Your sisters were witnesses to it.

The P. I. exhaled a puff of smoke in his client's face.

-What the- what the hell was that?

Edward put down his cigarette. The room had gone pitch black.

-I'm not sure. The sun-

Edward turned to face the window. He got up and walked toward it, leaned on the window sill and gazed upward at what had been a dark, blue sky. It was now a black sky, but like nothing any living being in recorded history had ever seen. The stars and distant galaxies were visible against the pure backdrop of infinite space. The moon could be seen, but only as a new moon barely perceptible against the night sky. It was to have been a

full moon that night, but there was no light being reflected off its surface. The sun had vanished from the sky.

-Miss Estravades?

-i'm sorry. What were you asking? Are we almost finished? I have some Christmas shopping to do.

-You and Mr. Mendez left the ice rink that night and came directly here?

-Yes.

-Why?

-I don't understand your question.

-Why come here, Miss Estravades, when your own apartment is only a few blocks away from the skating rink?

-We had already planned on seeing Marlena. We'd been invited to dinner, so why shouldn't we come here?

Yolanda could see that he didn't believe her. Had she said too much? Did she sound scared?

-Whose car did you use?

Yolanda hadn't been prepared for this pretty obvious question. It had slipped her mind.

-Miss Estravades? Did you use your boyfriend's car?

-No. We used Dolores' car. I'll bet you already knew that.

Lt. Donovan ignored the question.

-Really? You had the keys to her car?

-Yes. Dolores gave me an extra set just in case I needed to use it.

-So…Miss Sarney left the ice rink just past sunset without telling you and without taking her own car. Why?

-I don't know. She probably went shopping at Macy's or someplace near the garment district. She worked there, you know.

-I know. So, you left your girlfriend stranded. What was the big hurry? What were you and Mr. Mendez running away from?

-From nothing.

-Did you kill Dolores Sarney?

Yolanda was on the point of tears. Maybe, she should cry. Would tears move this detective?

-No! I had no motive to kill her. That's what you need to kill someone, isn't it?

Lt. Donovan nodded.

-That and the means and the opportunity. But, murder can be a lot more complicated than just motive. There are lots of reasons why people are bumped off.

-Are we almost finished?

-Did your boyfriend kill Miss Sarney?

-No. He didn't. He only met her once and that was the day before. And, Dolores and I were best friends. I even loaned her the money to buy her car. She was always broke. Her job didn't pay much.

-Lady, that's the first statement you made that I can make book on. Do you know who killed Miss Sarney? I want you to think about that one for just a second.

Yolanda answered too quickly.

-No. I've no idea.

-Did you make any side trips before coming to Miss Lake's residence that night?

-We came straight here. It was pouring rain that night. I'll never forget it.

-And, you stayed the night?

-You know that we didn't. You're trying to trick me.

-You booked a flight to Berlin, Germany that same evening. Care to tell me why?

-It was on impulse. Marlena was going and she invited me and Edward to come along.

A new hardness entered Lt. Donovan's voice. He was losing patience real fast. He knew this broad was holding out on him.

-Those tickets were purchased at the airport only minutes before take off, except yours and your boyfriend's. Yours and Mr. Mendez's tickets had been purchased hours before. Why was that, Miss Estravades? Marlena Lake and her party were joining you and Mr. Mendez and not the other way around. You visited Berlin and, then, Cairo, Egypt. Why? I can't hear you. *Why*?

Yolanda got up and walked over to the window. Dusk was settling in but a few car windows were still reflecting the sun's rays.

-Stalling, Miss Estravades?

Yolanda was about to turn on the detective when, in an instant, the sun's light was gone and the street was pitch black.

-Oh my God! Did you see that?

Lt. Donovan had seen it. The light in the sky had gone out. He hurried over to the closed window and flung it open.

-What the hell happened to the sun?

-You're asking me? Everything just went black. Look! The street lamps are starting to come on. Thank God!

-This is insane. It's not a blackout. The lights in the house are still on. This makes no sense. I'd better call the station. Is there a phone I can use?

He looked about the room for one.

-Of course. But, are they likely to know anything? I don't think so.

-Is there a radio you can turn on? There may be something on the news.

-There's one over here.

Yolanda pointed to a radio console in the far corner of the room. She went over to turn it on. Static. She tried every radio station.

-I can't raise anything on it. If Marlena were here, maybe she could.

-I'd like to meet Miss Lake. She sounds like quite a character.

-Good evening, Detective.

Lt. Donovan stopped dialing and put down the phone's receiver. Marlena Lake was standing in the doorway.

-And, good evening to you, Miss Lake.

The two of them were looking at each other with recognition in their eyes; there was no mistaking it. That man and this…woman? Her face was distorted. Her features were uneven.

Susan picked up her briefcase and walked toward the exit without looking back. She reached the glass door and pulled it open. And, then, the sky went black.

-What in the world…

People stopped dead in their tracks and gazed upward at the sky while others were bumping into each other in fear and confusion. The street lamps came flickering on. Drivers were reckless: jumping lights, zig-zagging to get ahead of any vehicle in front of them. Panic was spreading.

Susan was one of the first to recover from the initial shock of the phenomenon. She weaved her way through the crowd, holding on to her briefcase. She reached the corner of 42nd St. and 5th Ave. and looked for a cab. It wasn't easy spotting one in the darkness. The street lamps weren't that much help because their light couldn't cope with the unnatural blackness.

Susan glanced back to make certain that she wasn't being followed. She *was* being followed. The man and woman were coming toward her…staring her down. She ran across the street and was almost run down by a speeding car. She was lucky, but the car wasn't. It crashed into the downtown bus causing a massive traffic jam.

The young woman walked as fast as she could: dodging people when some of them walked right into her and others who wanted to actually stop and talk about the nightmare in the sky. She was close to panic, but she held on to her composure.

Susan reached the corner of 43rd St. and 5th Ave.. She had to stop and wait for the traffic light to turn. It gave her a chance to catch her breath. Her eyes were starting to adjust to the darkness. Dare she turn around to look? She did. That same man and woman were almost upon her. She ran across the street. Her pursuers were behind her and not more than ten feet away. My God! Was that woman's face coming off? Had she been wearing a mask to hide some disfigurement or something even worse?

Susan reached 44th St. and 5th. No! The light turned red. She couldn't just stand still and let them catch up to her. She started down 44th St. heading east. And, then, she saw a cab.

-Taxi!

Susan shouted out the word as a typical New Yorker. She didn't wait for it to stop. She ran into the street, rapped on the taxi's hood and flung open the door and jumped in.

-Please, step on it.

-Lady, you live dangerously. Where to?

-East 90th off 1st Ave. Now, please, don't stop for anyone else.

-You're the boss.

-Hurry before the light changes.

-Whatever you say.

Susan turned to face the window. The woman's face was right up against the glass. She screamed. The driver floored the accelerator and the taxi shot down the street.

Susan stared disbelievingly at the window. What had been the woman's "face" was still there, smeared on to the glass. Her curiosity got the best of her. She tried cranking the window open wanting to see what that mask was made of. She got the window halfway down and reached outside to grab what remained of the woman's "face", but it fell off before she could grab any part of it. All that remained was a cosmetic smear. She closed the window.

They just made the next light when Susan caught sight of her pursuers. She leaned back in the cab's seat and put her briefcase next to her. She caught a glimpse of her refection in the cab's rear view mirror. Her blonde hair was pulled back with a red ribbon. She tightened the ribbon because it was coming loose.

-Hey, Miss, you know what's up?

-You mean the sudden darkness?

-Like the sun just dropping out of the sky like that. Is this one of those eclipses?

-That's not a far fetched theory, actually. I hadn't thought of it.

-But, don't those things just last a couple of minutes?

-How long has it been? I've lost track of the time. Surely, more than three minutes must have passed.

-It's gotta' be at least ten minutes; maybe a little more than that.

-Then, it can't be an eclipse. If that were true, it would mean that the moon was virtually stopped in its orbit. I hope that's not the case.

-Why not, lady?

-If the moon were to slow down in its orbit, it would collide with the earth or be ripped to pieces by the earth's gravity. It would mean the end of the world.

-Sorry I asked.

-No. I'm sure it's not an eclipse. It was too sudden.

-You're the brainy type. I can tell. You a college professor or something?

Susan smiled at these questions. They were harmless and good-natured, not like that woman interrogator of a few minutes ago.

-No. Just a bit of a would-be scholar.

-So, how come you playing chicken with taxi cabs? Risky business, that.

-Believe it or not, I was being followed.

-Why wouldn't I believe it? I'd believe anything in this town. Do you know why they were tailing you?

-I don't. Well, I have a vague idea, but nothing really concrete.

-I'm gonna head on up to 57th and go cross town from there. Is that okay with you?

-Sounds good to me just as long as I get home. I've got a few questions for my darling mother.

-You think maybe she knows anything about what's goin' on?

Susan undid the top button of her trench coat.

-It wouldn't surprise me in the least.

Nella Mendez was about to enter her mother's bed-room. She was the second youngest of five children and had been unofficially delegated as their bedridden mother's caregiver. Her elder sister, Victoria, did help out with the maternal chores, but the main duties fell at Nella's feet.

Nella loved her home and stayed close to it and the immediate neighborhood. Infrequently, she would venture into Manhattan to purchase a book that was not available from the public library or drop in at one of the department stores to browse. She was a loving daughter and a steadfast sister who had helped to raise her kid brother, Edward. She was quite proud of him. And, she was keen on meeting his new girlfriend, the ice skater. It was strange that Edward hadn't yet brought her over to the house.

She entered her mother's bedroom.

-I've brought you your dinner tray, mother. Would you like me to stay and keep you company while you eat? I can read to you, if you like. Here. I'll fix your pil-low.

-Stop fussing, Nella.

-Did I hear you speaking to someone just now?

-You did not. And, I've not yet acquired the habit of speaking to myself.

Why was Nella hesitating to ask her question? Why on this day had she chosen to broach that particular sub-ject?

-What time is it?

-Nearly four o'clock.

-Why am I having my dinner so early?

-It's your tea, mother. I wasn't thinking when I said "dinner" before.

-Not thinking and your usual imaginings. One could almost mistake you for the invalid.

-Indeed. Mother...Victoria and I visited the church where you and father were married: Queen of All Saints. It was quite lovely: almost like a cathedral.

Isabelle Mendez looked at her youngest daughter with cold and blackened eyes that held mistrust in them. She didn't favor Nella with her distrust; she resented the entire world with one or two exceptions. She, like her youngest daughter, was fond of books and knowledge. Mrs. Mendez actually felt a pang of maternal guilt at having cut short her daughter's college education. She wanted her daughters close to her to protect them from the evil in the world that could not be seen and this protective instinct extended even to the rebellious Dottie who had dared to have a life of her own. Mrs. Mendez also had a fear of being left alone in the house.

-Mother, did you hear me?

-I heard you. And, how I have grown to distrust you and your meddlesome sister, Victoria. Hate me, Nella. You should, you know. I would if in your place. You're fishing for information and don't deny it. Catrina tells me everything that you and your three sisters do.

-My sister, Catrina, knows nothing of what I do.

-You think so? Then, you are the fool. I'll tell you nothing that you want to know because you already know nothing. Count yourself fortunate.

-Mother, since you are aware of my motives, what does the symbol of a spear mean to you? Am I being direct enough with you now?

-A spear?

The old woman whispered the word in a broken utterance.

-Yes. A spear. I dreamt of one last night. It took place in the church where you and father were married: that was the reason for my and Victoria's visit today.

-In what context was this dream of yours? Tell me. I must know.

-A young man was being sacrificed upon the altar. The spear was driven through his heart. As it happens, I actually met this young man when he was a young boy.

-When was this?

-It was twenty-three years ago. I remember the date because it was around the time of Edward's Holy Communion.

-Who was this young boy? Had you also known his parents?

-His name was Werner Hoffman. His adoptive parents were killed on that day; perhaps, murdered would be a more appropriate term.

-The storm! The unholy storm that had not been seen for two thousand years. I remember that day. How could one forget it? Terrifying! Edward and I were in the house by ourselves on that day.

-And, that in itself is strange. Mother, what does it all mean? I do have an interest in the occult. I've even purchased some books from that dreadful book shop on 18th St. in Manhattan.

Mrs. Mendez put down her teacup.

-You've been there? You've been to that evil place? Don't go back, Nella. People have been murdered in that accursed place. Black masses have been held there in the back room.

-I'm not surprised. Was father an occultist?

-What if he was? Does it matter? Let the dead stay buried with their secrets. Go about your mundane life, Nella, and forget about these things. It is the one piece of maternal advice that I can give you. I was warned to stay away from such things myself, for it was forbidden to me in this lifetime. And, in a manner of speaking, I heeded that advice; but, not as I should have.

-I think I understand. So, you married an occultist.

It was not a question.

-My pride and vanity would not keep me away from the occult. The pull was too strong for me to resist. You must do what I could not.

-My interest is an intellectual one, mother.

-Do not go beyond that boundary. And, do not frequent that book shop, again. It should be burned to the ground and salt poured into the foundation.

-You're frightened. For the first time in my life, I see fear in your eyes.

-I won't deny it; but this is not the first time that I have felt fear What books have you read?

-Mother! You're incorrigible. I've only read-

Isabelle Mendez looked past her youngest daughter. What she saw took her breath away.

-Mother, what is it? You're trembling.

-Nella! Outside the window…look! The light has gone from the sky.

-What are you saying?

Nella rushed over to the window and opened it. The sun had vanished.

CHAPTER THREE

EDWARD TRIED keeping one eye on the nightmarish scene unfolding outside his office building and the other eye on his new client, Werner Hoffman, Jr. It wasn't easy. Yes. Edward was staring at the man standing next to him who in turn was staring at the private investigator. Not exactly a Mexican stand-off, just one man sizing up another, trying to read the other's character.

And, after a few real long moments, Edward turned his gaze away from the phenomenon outside his building to give his full attention to his client who was standing just a little too close to him.

-Maybe, he wants to push me out the window? You never can tell. He'll have a broken neck if he tries anything.

Aloud, Edward spoke to his client.

-Okay, Mr. Hoffman, what gives? Level with me, pal. What do you know about what's going on out there? Hold up. I'll rephrase that question: what the fuck has happened to the damned sun? Forgive the vulgarity, but give. And, don't lie to me. I get real mad when people do that.

-What are you asking of me?

-I'm asking you for the truth.

Edward thought back for a second to what his sister, Nella, had once told him: the truth is indestructible.

-I've no idea, Mr. Mendez. I swear. How could I possibly know? I'm as shocked as you seem to be.

Edward decided that he didn't like his new client which meant that he sure didn't trust him.

-Sit down. And, I don't believe you. You look concerned, but not all that surprised. Look, pal, no sun! You're not even sweating anymore.

The two men sat back down in their respective chairs. Edward leaned across his desk, took out another cigarette and pointed it at Werner Hoffman, Jr.

-Okay...Werner, tell me your story from the beginning up to the here and the now. Let's have it. And, by the way, I like long stories. I might have told you that already. Details are essential in my business. I might have mentioned that, too.

He glanced back at the window. Christ! It looked like eternal night out there: it was a pretty horrifying sight. He lit his cigarette. Was his hand shaking?

The P. I.'s new client began his tale.

-Just the other night, I stood for a long time in Battery Park and stared into the bay's waters. The night air was cold, but the sky was clear. The wind was sharp and not even my woolen scarf could keep the chill out. I had no place to go except to an empty apartment. Perhaps, it was symbolic of an empty life.

-Your life sounds pretty interesting to me.

-Perhaps.

-Where do you call home?

-On the upper west side on Broadway and 72nd St.

Edward tried keeping the sarcasm out of his voice.

-Sorry to interrupt. You were saying?

-It was on the morning of my Holy Communion that I first met my biological father. It was a beautiful spring day. The sun was like a golden disc hurled into the azure sky by an ancient god. My mother had dressed me in a navy blue suit and my adoptive father placed a white carnation in my jacket's lapel. I grew fearful and cold despite the warmth of the day and kept taking off my spectacles for no good reason.

-At what point, Mr. Hoffman, did your real father come into the picture?

-He was standing in the alleyway by the church. He was well dressed and properly groomed. He walked toward me and extended his hand. I was standing on the communion line just outside church with my fellow classmates. The line moved forward and I with it. I lost sight of him.

-When did you see him, again?

-After Mass. I was outside the church and he was standing there with my parents. They introduced me to Mr. Werner Hoffman. He had told them that he was a friend of a friend who had known my mother in her youth. He had been abroad for a long time and now he wanted to pick up the thread of a life left behind in this country.

-Not a bad story. Almost cozy, if you get my drift.

-Yes. A convenient story not easily checked if one were to go to that length.

-Where did the four of you take off from there?

-We went to an Italian restaurant in the neighborhood. I remember looking up at the sky, Mr. Mendez. It looked like an ocean of blue-green sea foam whose waters were etheric and soft to the touch...like an angel's wings.

-Uh-huh.

-The restaurant was small and dimly lit. Mr. Hoffman, my father, ordered for everyone. And, Mr. Mendez, your sisters were sitting across the room from us; although, I did not know their identity at the time.

Edward put out his cigarette in the glass ashtray. It was a gift from his sister, Dottie, who was also a heavy smoker.

-What? Are you joking? How long ago was this, pal? You were seven years old, right? What are you now?

-I am thirty.

-Okay. So, we're talking twenty-three years past which would bring us back to 1924. Keep talking.

-My father whispered to me that I must be obedient and do what I was told without question. He would never mistreat me, but the demands and sacrifices would be great.

-Was your father a Nazi? Don't be offended, but it's the impression I'm getting.

-I'm not offended. Yes. He was a Nazi, but not at that moment in time. You are perceptive.

-How the hell did I guess?

-He told me to study those ladies at the table, Mr. Mendez, your sisters. He described them as being pedestrian. I hope I do not offend you. My father said that they might have information and clues that they, themselves, were unaware of.

-Clues to what? Would it be that spear you want me to find? My sisters are a helluva' lot more interesting than I thought.

Edward played with the ash of his extinguished cigarette.

-There must have been a purpose to that luncheon.

-My father spoke highly of your sister, Nella: an educated woman with some exposure to university. He didn't like your eldest sister, Catrina.

Edward laughed.

-No one does. She's a self-centered bitch.

-My father observed Catrina's mannerisms as affectations. Her clothes and style of make-up were "starched." Her opinions were short-sighted and shallow.

-Okay, pal. I know who my sisters are. Were Dottie and Victoria there, too?

-Yes. All were present. It was Dottie who brought up the subject of secrets that involved your mother and eldest sister. She mentioned the "big" secret: the one that has been kept under the rug, so to speak.

Edward reached into his coat pocket.

-Cigarette? Gum?

-It's your last cigarette.

Edward made like a cigarette advertisement.

-I've got another pack. See? Luckies.

-No. Thank you. A stick of gum would be nice, though.

-Here.

Hoffman took the stick of gum.

-Your sister, Catrina, would not speak of this secret. She appeared nervous and refused to speak to anyone from that moment on. A strange reaction, no?

-I'll bet. My mother and Catrina have always been thick as thieves. They tolerate the rest of us. Whatever it is they share, it's on the dark and unholy side. I'd make bet on that.

-When the four of us left the restaurant, the day had darkened and the wind had picked up. I'd never seen clouds so black and massive. They looked solid. It was so dark that the street lamps had been turned on…much like today. Streaks of lightning appeared in the sky. The sound of that lightning was like electric currents scraping along the sides of the buildings. My father shouted for us to take cover or we would be killed with my adoptive parents. He said that it had been ordained and we were powerless to stop it.

-Ordained? By whom? God?

-To this day, I don't know. We ran as fast as we could when the rains were unleashed from the black horrors above us. We tried to avoid the panic stricken people: drivers and pedestrians were not responding well to this phenomenon. They should have known that the storm's intensity could not endure for long.

Edward played with the pack of Luckies.

-Panic is a pretty dangerous thing. We might be getting some of that about now. What happened to your adoptive parents?

-They were killed by the lightning.

-Not a nice way to die.

-I directed my father to our apartment house. The two of us ran up the stoop. He fumbled in his coat pocket for the keys that he'd stolen form my adoptive father.

-A Nazi and a thief. Figures.

-We entered the building and climbed the stairs in the dark hallway not realizing that there'd been a power outage in the area. My father tried frantically to unbolt the apartment door.

"Why is the damned key not turning in the lock? Mustn't be the right key. I stole the wrong key!"

"You are jamming the lock. Let me have a try before you break it."

Edward interrupted the narrative. He had an uneasy feeling in his gut.

-Who was doing the talking: a tenant in the building, a friend of your parents?

-We nearly jumped out of our skins at the sound of that feminine voice. We hadn't noticed her because Marlena Lake hadn't wanted to be noticed. She took the key from my father's hand and gently shoved it into the lock. The door opened with a soft click.

"My name is Marlena Lake. I'm a friend of this boy's mother. You don't know me, Werner. How could you? I live in Manhattan and I thought I might drop by and pay my respects to-"

"That's very interesting, Miss Lake, but-"

"-to congratulate this young man on his Holy Communion. The parents are not here. Have they been detained unexpectedly or was it planned? Tell me."

"Who are you? Never mind. Please, get out of my way. I don't have to answer any of your questions."

"I've told you my name. Would you now return the favor?"

"Good day, Miss Lake. I've no time for this nonsense."

"I'll wait downstairs in the vestibule until this rather dreadful storm has subsided. It reminds me of the storm after the Crucifixion. It reminds me of His murder. I believe the veil of the temple was rent in half. We pay for our crimes."

Again, Edward interrupted his client's narrative.

-Marlena Lake…this gets curiouser and curiouser. Brother, you've got my undivided attention. What the hell was she up to that day?

- I don't know. But, before I could say anything, my father shoved me into the apartment and slammed the door shut. He flung some of my clothes into a briefcase and we left. Much to my father's annoyance, Miss Lake was waiting for us downstairs.

"Should I expect the boy's parents home soon or have they been delayed?

Werner Hoffman's smile was not a nice one.

"No. You should not expect them home at all."

"Why not?

"None of your damned business."

"You may have much to answer for. What has happened to the parents? You must know."

"What makes you think that anything has happened to them? And, I'll take my chances. Now, get out of my way."

"We'll meet, again, you ill-mannered bastard. This is not the end by any means."

"Don't count on it."

Edward sat back in his chair and let out a long trail of cigarette smoke. He'd found another pack of cigarettes in one of the desk drawers.

-Is there much more to your story; and where does the spear come into it?

-No. It won't take too much longer.

Edward was about to put his feet up on his desk, but stopped himself.

-I'm not rushing you; but, I need to make a phone call. It'll take only a minute.

The P. I. picked up the phone's receiver but there was no dial tone.

-What the- The phone lines must have been affected. All I'm getting is static.

He put the receiver back in its cradle.

-Go on with your story, Werner.

-Miss Lake attended my parent's wake as did your sister, Miss Nella. Your sisters had heard the dying screams of my parents and rushed out of the restaurant to see if they could help, but there was nothing that anyone could do. My parents were already dead. The Italian waiters brought the two dead people into the waiting area of the restaurant. I believe it was your sister, Nella, who summoned the police.

-Why on earth would my sister, Nella, go to your adoptive parents' wake?

-I don't know. I did see Miss Lake speaking to your sister at the wake. She told Miss Nella that she had foreseen my adoptive parents' death through the Tarot cards. My mother had asked her for a reading the night before.

-Your mother knew Marlena Lake? How? *Why*? What would Marlena be doing in that part of Brooklyn?

Your tale gets more bizarre by the second. How did the two women come to know each other? Marlena had to have had a reason. She doesn't have casual friendships.

-I remember Miss Lake's words and your sister's. They are ingrained on my memory.

-Give.

Marlena Lake looked directly into Nella Mendez's eyes.

"We all have our secrets, but I'll tell you one of mine, Miss Mendez. I saw their deaths through the Tarot cards. They were murdered...eliminated. Little Werner's mother had had a premonition in a dream: a premonition of her own death and that of her husband's. We were becoming friends because that poor woman was lonely and desperate. At one point, she had been my housekeeper. She was good at her job and I was sorry to lose her.

Nella Mendez fumbled in her pocketbook for a handkerchief as Marlena continued to address her.

"I see people for what they are and not what they claim to be. That man who is sitting with the boy? He's being hunted down by others who seek him out. Their methods of execution are not pretty. He's being used and doesn't have the good sense to know it; but, in time he will.

"Do you have a family, Miss Mendez?"

"Of course. Why do you ask?"

"They are involved, as well as yourself."

"Involved in what? I've no idea what you're talking about."

"Haven't you?"

"I don't care to hear anymore. Your talking in riddles."

"As you wish. But, you may regret that decision. Here is my card. Don't hesitate to contact me. We may have quite a bit to talk about."

Nella nodded toward Werner Hoffman.

"Is that man now the boy's legal guardian?"

"So he claims. And, who is there to stop him? Who would want to stop him?"

"Should he be stopped, Miss Lake?"

"The game should be played out to the end."

Edward leaned almost too far back in his chair.

-Marlena Lake is always playing some dangerous game. And, damn it! I've gotta' have a long talk with my sister, Nella, tonight. She actually *met* Marlena.

Hoffman continued his story as if the P. I. had not interrupted. Edward took note of this because it had the ring of a rehearsed speech.

-The next day, we boarded the ship for Europe. We traveled second class, a most uncomfortable way to travel at that time.

-Your father didn't waste any time, did he? That was the day of the funeral, wasn't it? He had it all figured out, didn't he?

-Yes to all of those pointed questions. We arrived in Germany on an overcast day. We reached Berlin a few days later by train. From that moment on, I was to speak only German. We stopped in a cafeteria for some food and to get our bearings. My father met a friendly waitress by the name of Henrietta who helped us to find a one bedroom flat in her building. The rent was reasonable and there was even a refrigerator in the kitchen. We took a look at the place that day and paid a month's rent in advance.

Hoffman took a drag on his cigarette.

-But, our first day in Berlin was not yet over. I was to meet a Frenchwoman that night: an old friend of my father's. It was from her that I first learned of the Spear of Longinus. Her name was Nathalie Montaigne. She was petite and heavily made-up. I didn't like her. About her, there was a hardness despite the outward charm. This is how their conversation went.

"Werner! My God! Give Nathalie a kiss, please. Ah! A cold, German kiss. What else could I expect?"

"I'd like you to meet my son, Werner. I brought him back with me from America."

"Your son! I can see the resemblance. Handsome like his father. But, let us sit down. We have much to discuss. May I talk freely in front of the boy?"

"He is one of us, Nathalie."

"How delicious! When did you arrive in Berlin?

"This morning. And, as you can see, we're still un-packing."

"And, how quickly you found these rooms. Am I the first to be an honored guest? Flatter my vanity, dear Werner."

"Of course."

"So, let us talk shop. How goes it, if you get my drift."

"It still has not been found. I feel the pressure of the Party's impatience. Makes me feel like a hunted animal."

"I understand. It is not fair for any of us. But, once we find it our future and position will be assured. They must be or else."

"Yes? Or else what?"

"If they betray us, they will pay dearly for it. I promise this on all the saints."

"A funny thing to make a promise on."

"I know. But, one never ceases to be a Catholic." She looked about the room. "Are there no chairs to sit on?"

"You were saying?"

Nathalie put her pocketbook on the floor.

"The rise to power can be swift, but the fall can be equally devastating. What can be given can be taken away."

"And, the consequences for us?"

"Deadly. I am no fool, cherie. But, one plays with life and death every day, no? Here. I will sit on the window sill." She made herself comfortable and continued. "No one wishes to die, but it's a fate that we all share. So...tell Nathalie, where do you think it is?"

"I believe the spear is in America. Manuel Mendez knew the secret. He possessed the spear for a long time and was the last to have it. It disappeared upon his death. Holderman-

"That pig! I hate him. Not to be trusted.

"Agreed. He couldn't find the spear."

"So he says. Lies come quite easily to his kind."

"Mendez's youngest daughter may help us to find it...or should I say that she may guide young Werner here to its location. She actually attended the parents' wake."

"Excellent. But, this woman-"

"Can be dealt with."

Edward pointed his cigarette at Hoffman.

-I don't like the sound of that. That's my sister your father was talking about. She practically raised me. So, your father knew my father. That's not a question, by the way.

-Yes. My story is almost finished. When I grew to be fifteen, my father confided to me several things. We were in a crowded bistro and no one was paying any attention to us.

Edward grinned.

-You hope. Let me just fill you in on something, pal: in a public place, someone is *always* listening in on your conversation. Always.

"Werner, after the Great War, our country was devastated. I didn't know what to do with myself, so I began a search for like-minded people who were interested in the occult. Not an easy task. One day, in the back room of a bar, I met Nathalie Montaigne. She had ideas and was willing to share her bed with me and also some of her ideas and contacts. It was a fortunate meeting."

Edward took out his notepad and began making notes.

-Mr. Mendez, my father was frightened by what he was telling me. It was as if he were taking a chance by telling this to his own son.

-Keep talking. I'd like to know what else your dad had to say.

"Many years ago, a sacred article was either stolen or lost; hard to say which. It was the Spear of Longinus which may one day be humanity's last hope for survival.

"The spear, Werner, has a long and dark history. It was first recorded as the spear that pierced the side of the Christ. However, it and the Roman soldier go back much further than any man can guess. That same spear was once the staff of Moses, a practitioner of the black arts if ever there was one. That estimable magician learned his craft from the very gods of Egypt: the gods of the heavens who had descended to Earth millennia ago. The spear, though, is even more ancient than the oldest civilization for it was fashioned from the Tree of Life that once grew in the not-so-fabled Garden.

"Werner, soon there will be another war even more horrific than the first. Entire cities will be destroyed in a maelstrom of fire. Try to survive if you can and make your way back to America. I have contacts there and they can help you."

"Father, you sound as if you-"

"When the war is over, go to New York City. I will give you the names of people to contact." He gripped his son's hand. "Werner, we have been betrayed by our own Party. It was you who I was told would find the spear. A lie. In fact, I'm certain that it has not only been found, but put to use. Just take a good look around you: look at the upheaval in Europe and look at the cause of it all."

"Who betrayed us?"

"That pig, Holderman. I'm certain of it. Don't ask me anymore. It's not good to talk about past treachery. Admittedly, we have been compensated, but not enough."

"Please, go on. What are we to do now?"

"Survive the coming war and, then, return to America. The spear will be taken from the Chancellor; make no mistake of that. Only the initiated may possess it and even then for only short periods of time. The spear belongs to no one. Even Manuel Mendez, an egotist if ever there was one, had to concede that."

For a couple of seconds, the P. I. turned his back on Hoffman. He stared out the window…a window whose pane of glass looked like it was covered over with black paint. He moved his chair a couple of inches and now he could see a few lights on in the building across the street: these lights looked like solid blocks of white set into black stone.

Edward turned around to look into his new client's blue eyes. He closed his notepad. It had all sounded like some well-crafted speech given by a shrewd politician: a mixture of lies, truth, and hints.

-That's some story, pal.

-It is all true. I survived the war by working for the Ministry of Propaganda. I was good at my job, although you wouldn't like very much what I did.

-And, what about your dad? Did he survive the war?

-He is dead.

Edward noted the evasive answer.

-So, in 1932 when you were a young teenager, he took you into his confidence. It turns out that this Holderman just might have snatched the spear. Tell me if I'm getting it right.

-You are.

-Then, taking you from your adoptive parents turned out to be-

-Pointless, Mr. Mendez.

Edward heard the steam coming up through the pipes: a loud clanging and hissing sound. He got up

from his desk and turned on the overhead lights. Up to this point, the only light on in the dark office had been the desk lamp.

-That's better. I'm kind of surprised the heat's coming up on a Sunday afternoon. Must be getting pretty cold out there.

-Yes. It must. With the sun gone, Mr. Mendez we will soon all be dead on a frozen planet.

-The sun is gone? Vanished? How do you know that? It might be some kind of eclipse.

-I believe it to be so. I saw no sun on the horizon when looking out your window a few moments ago. It is no eclipse that we are witnessing.

-You sound pretty sure about that. Let's try the radio. Maybe that's working.

Edward walked over to the window sill where he kept his portable radio. He switched it on.

-Nothing but static.

He switched off the radio.

-Mr. Mendez? About the spear?

-What about it?

-Can you help me locate it?

-I'm willing to bet that I can. You've given me a starting point. By the way, Werner, what does this spear look like? Any idea, pal?

-I'm not certain. The shaft, I believe, is made of wood.

-And, the point?

-A metallic alloy.

-Fair enough.

-And, your fee, Mr. Mendez? You'll require a retainer's fee.

-Three hundred up front and twenty-five a day, plus expenses. How does that sound?

Hoffman withdrew a billfold from his suit jacket, counted out three one hundred dollar bills a twenty and a fiver and handed them over to the P. I..

-You carry a lot of cash around with you. You might just want to open up a checking account for yourself. Let me make out a receipt for you.

-I plan on doing so tomorrow when the banks are open.

The P. I. got his receipt book out.

-I'll get started on this right away. Do you have a business card for me?

-Here.

Edward examined the card.

-By the way, had my sister, Nella, spoken about me? Here's your receipt.

Hoffman pocketed the receipt without looking at it.

-Thank you. I knew of you. Your sister and I have never had an actual conversation as I was only a child at the time.

Hoffman glanced out the window.

- I must leave now. May I give you a lift if you're going uptown?

He stood up and put on his overcoat.

-No. Thanks. I've got my own car; but, I'm tempted to leave it where it is which I've done for the past couple of days: playing parking tag with the cops. Anyway, I think the subway might be faster and safer.

Edward took a look out the window.

-Man, is it dark out there. Better be careful driving.

-Good day, Mr. Mendez.

-I'll close up shop here and ride the elevator down with you.

-As you wish.

Edward closed the window and switched off the lights. The office had never been so pitch black. He threw on his leather jacket and got a hold of his hat: a gift from Yolanda.

Once outside, the two men stood in the building's doorway giving their eyes a chance to adjust to the un-natural darkness. No one was about, but they could hear the sound of traffic up on Chambers St.

-Look at the sky, Mr. Mendez. One can see the stars so clearly; a magnificent sight, no?

Hoffman put his hat on.

-It's a pretty impressive sight, all right; but, I prefer a nice, subtle sunset.

Hoffman put on his gloves.

-The air feels much colder than it did earlier this afternoon.

-It's like being stuck naked in an icebox. Where's your car, Werner?

-Right here in front of your building. Are you sure that I can't drop you off someplace?

-Nope. The subway's right around the corner.
They shook hands and went their separate ways.

CHAPTER FOUR

WERNER HOFFMAN got into his rented car and started the engine. He eased out of his parking spot and headed uptown. Had he been convincing? Had he mixed his lies with enough truth to satisfy the P. I.? He didn't know. The interview had not been easy and the celestial phenomenon that had taken place had not helped matters.. The P. I. had been sharp witted, had never taken his eyes off of him and had almost made the ultimate connection.

Edward turned the corner, but stopped just short of the subway kiosk. His thoughts were:

-Okay, pal, nice of you to point your car out to me. I think I'll do a bit of tail-gating. You're up to something. Hope Mr. Werner catches a red light.

Edward walked over to his parked car: a two door '46 Ford. He liked his new car: the black exterior and the muted gray interior. It was a clean and simple make that got 15 to 20 to the gallon in the city. The front had two bucket seats and a full back seat area that could accommodate up to three passengers and the trunk was sizable. The AC radio was Edward's favorite feature.

The P. I. started up his car and drove around the corner just in time to see the light change in Werner Hoffman's favor. Edward pressed harder on the gas pedal and made the light just in time.

-Close. Now, we'll just see where you're headed for.

The P. I. stayed about a half block behind his client's car. Normally, he wouldn't tail someone this close, but it was so dark out that anything moving between the illumination of the street lamps was lost from sight. He noticed that the illumination coming from his headlights looked almost solid: like vanilla ice cream spilling out of a cone. His thoughts went back to the car he was tailing.

-Thanks, Werner. You've turned this into one helluva' interesting day. You almost took my mind off that blonde chick in the subway car and that's saying something.

He glanced down at the dashboard.

-Let's see if I can raise anything on the radio.

He turned the dial and the dashboard lit up.

-Static. Damn it! What the hell's going on? Wait. Something's coming through.

He tried "fiddling" with the station indicator: there was static, but he could just about make out the gist of the announcer's words:

"At approximately four o'clock this afternoon, eastern time, a celestial phenomenon took place: it appears that the sun has vanished from the sky. In an instant, it was gone from sight. Scientists from around the globe are calling for an emergency conference to take place at the United Nations in New York City. Many feel that the current situation is dire. Without the sun's thermal heat the earth's-"

The radio transmission was cut-off.

Edward reached into the car's glove compartment and took out a pack of Lucky Strike. He unwrapped the cellophane and tore off the silver wrapping. His client ran into a red light up ahead.

-Good. Gives me time to light up.

He put the lit match to his cigarette and, then, tossed the match out the car's window.

-Needed that. I'm no scientist, but how is it that without a sun to warm our butts, the whole friggin' planet's not encased in a block of ice?

He shook his head. He noticed that the red light up ahead never looked more distinct and red. It looked suspended in mid-air and even the lights from the nearby buildings looked like suspended white squares in some absurd checker board pattern.

He couldn't help but laugh.

-Disaster does have its artistic side.

The light turned green and, once again, both cars were moving uptown on the west side. The traffic was picking up but moving slowly.

-Must be an accident up ahead. Wouldn't be surprised in all this mayhem.

Without warning, Hoffman's car veered left on to 18th St. He slowed down to park and Edward was forced to pass him. The P. I. couldn't stop because there were cars right behind him.

-Damn it! Wasn't expecting him to make that turn off.

Edward speeded up, made it to the corner, and risked parking in front of a fire hydrant. He got out of his car and ran down the block trying to conceal himself as much as he could in the new darkness. He could just make out Hoffman going into a building. He made his way to that spot and it turned out to be a book shop.

-Just what I thought: a book shop. Well, I can't go in or stay out here, that's for sure. Hmm. I'm closer to Marlena's place than my own. My mother and sisters should be all right for the time being. Nella is sensible enough to stay in the house and keep the door locked.

Edward walked back to his car and looked about the area. He saw a lighted window and a woman leaning out. Her gaze was fixed at the sky. She was transfixed by what she saw and didn't notice the him looking up at her.

-People are staying inside and that's good. I'll drive by Yolanda's place and see if she's gone back to her apartment.

He had most of his things at his girlfriend's place even though he maintained an apartment out in Staten Island. For some forgotten reason, he didn't want to let go of that apartment even though he didn't like the semi-isolation: it was inconvenient and time consuming traveling into Manhattan from Staten Island. There had been talk of building a bridge into Brooklyn to ease the traffic and open access to the borough, but that didn't help him out any at the present time.

Edward walked back to his car. He was the only person on the sidewalk. The cars driving by were practically invisible except for the headlights which looked like darting circles of light. To be the only pedestrian on any street in a city like New York was a rare and unnerving experience. Edward preferred the company of strangers to isolation.

The taxi was at a standstill. Car horns were blasting and drivers were shouting obscenities at each other or at no one in particular.

-It's not gonna' happen, Miss. The cops are barricading 57th St. in both directions. Nobody's gettin' through.

-Can we head further uptown along Central Park West and take the crosstown road at 72nd St? It might be accessible.

-I think Columbus Circle is blocked off. That's the sense I'm gettin'. Tell ya' what: let's detour down to 23rd and head crosstown over to 1st Ave. from there.

-I'm willing to try anything at this point. Maybe, I should just get out and walk home.

-With things as they are? I wouldn't chance it. It might not be too safe.

Susan looked into the darkness and the circles of light surrounding the taxi.

-You're probably right. Things look a little scary out there.

The cab driver made an illegal U-turn and headed downtown toward 23rd St.

-Not that it's any of my business, but it looked to me like you were running away from someone.

-I was.

-Maybe, I oughta' drop you off at the police station.

-Please, don't. I just need to get home.

-You're the boss; but, the precinct might be a safer place. And-

-Yes?

-I'll bet a month's salary that we're being followed right this minute. Take a look behind you.

Susan turned around to look out the rear window. She could see the headlights of a car, but couldn't make out the occupants inside.

-How long have they been following us?

-I'd say for the past fifteen minutes or so…give or take.

-Can you lose them? Say, yes.

-I sure can.

Marlena Lake entered her living room carrying her oversized black, patent leather pocketbook. For once, thought Yolanda, she's wearing something halfway decent: a plain, black dress and matching pumps and even her hair was combed. No wonder the sun had disappeared.

-What can we do for you, Detective?

-Miss Lake? Dolores Sarney has been found dead.

-A pity. What has that to do with me?

-She was a friend of yours, wasn't she?

-What of it?

Marlena sat down on the sofa and started rummaging through her pocketbook which had seen far better days. Yolanda joined her on the couch. Lt. Donovan remained standing by the window.

-Marlena, have you seen what's happening outside? The sun is gone.

Without looking up from the interior of her pocketbook…

-I'm aware of it, Yolanda. Detective? You were saying?

-Miss Lake, when was the last time you saw Miss Sarney?

-I believe it was sometime back in April of this year at a place called Armstrong's. It's a bar and grill off Columbus Circle. I frequent the place quite often. They have excellent hamburgers.

-How was she, Miss Lake?

-I don't understand. She was her usual self: a bit self-contained, as always.

-Did she seem disturbed about anything?

-She did not.

-When did you see her, again?

-I did not see Dolores after that evening. I am not her keeper, Detective. And, haven't you far more important things to take up your time like this recent phenomenon?

-I'm investigating a homicide. Dolores Sarney was brutally murdered and, then, dumped into the East River. That, to me, lady, is important business.

-I can't offer you any help. Now, would you please leave? I've things to do.

-Like what?

-None of your damned business.

-Miss Lake, you went on a little trip the evening of Miss Sarney's disappearance?

-I did.

-Mind telling me what for?

-A holiday of sorts mixed with business.

-What kind of business?

-I am a scholar of ancient Western history. I often take trips abroad.

-Did Miss Sarney have any relatives or close friends, aside from Miss Estravades here?

-Not that I know of, but I assume that she had. Yolanda, here, could better answer that question.

Lt. Donovan closed his notepad.

-Don't leave town, Miss Lake. And, that goes for you, too, Miss Estravades. I'm not finished with either one of you. And, Miss Lake? watch that attitude.

He put his black notepad back in his jacket pocket and showed himself out.

Yolanda turned on Marlena.

-Why did you have to antagonize him like that? He could cause a lot of trouble for us.

Marlena closed her pocketbook.

-You worry too much. He doesn't know anything and has proof of nothing. We're not responsible for Dolores' death. The person responsible is dead.

-But, he thinks we *are* responsible.

-Let him think whatever the hell he wants to for all the good it'll do him. We've far more important things to worry about than some flatfoot. The world, my dear, may be coming to an end.

Marlena got up and went over to the window.

-Susan should have been home by now. What in the world is keeping her?

-Marlena, the sun…it just vanished. It's pitch black outside. It's terrifying!

Marlena's tone was grim as she turned to face the figure skater.

-I know.

-You're taking it pretty well. There might be panic in the streets. I wouldn't be surprised if there were. The phones aren't working.

-How bothersome.

-I tried calling Edward at his office, but I couldn't get through.

Marlena's mind was elsewhere as she once again stared out the window.

-Susan is quite capable and resourceful. She'll walk home if she must.

-How safe would that be? I wouldn't walk anywhere in that darkness. People go crazy when they panic or feel threatened.

-The street lamps have come on.

Marlena turned away from the window.

-But, you're right, my dear. It could be dangerous to walk alone in the streets just now.

-I couldn't get anything on the radio. Even Lt. Donovan tried to and couldn't raise anything.

-Let's try, again, shall we? Turn it on.

Yolanda went to the radio console and turned the switch on. There was static, but the announcer's voice could be heard.

-Yolanda, try to get it clearer. There! That's it. Now, turn the volume up.

"A state of emergency has been declared by the Mayor. All residents are urged to stay in their homes as public transportation is operating on a restricted basis. As far as authorities can tell, the recent "blackout" has not affected essential services, although radio and telephone transmissions have been disrupted. At this time, the President has called for an emergency meeting of his cabinet and details of that meeting will be forthcoming. Scientists from around the globe have been called to an emergency summit to be held at the United Nations.

"No explanation has yet been offered for the celestial phenomenon. The sun, it would appear, is no longer visible to the human eye. A few scattered reports have come in that where our sun once was…there is now a void in space. These reports have not yet been confirmed."

-Turn it off. The fools don't know a damned thing.

-Marlena?

-Yes?

-What do *you* know?

Marlena was saved the trouble of answering Yolanda's pointed question. The front door opened and Susan walked in.

-Thank you so much for everything-

-Fred.

-Fred. I've got your cab number. Now, please, be safe.

-Goodnight, Miss-

-Susan.

-Susan. Stay indoors and lock your door. And, if you need a reliable cab driver, ask for me.

-I will, Fred. And, thanks, again.

As soon as the cab driver left the lighting of the front door, he was lost in the darkness. Susan strained to see his retreating figure, but couldn't. She closed the front door and locked it.

-Susan? We're in the living room. Please, come in and join us.

The young woman took off her trench coat and hat and placed her briefcase on the end table in the foyer.

-Mother? Yolanda? I won't bother to ask if you've noticed things, but has there been any word on the radio? We couldn't raise anything on the cab's radio coming up.

-No one knows anything, Susan, or else they're just stalling for time before they level with us. Did you manage to take out the books I sent you for?

-They're in my briefcase. I left it in the hallway.

-Good girl. Was there much panic in the streets?

-Not as much as you might expect. But, one gets the feeling that that will change. It's all a bit unnerving. There were a few traffic accidents.

-Was that the cab driver I heard you speaking to?

-It was. A very gallant man by the name of Fred: a real New York gent.

-Was it wise to show him to the door?

-He literally saved my life, mother. I was being followed by two…things.

-Christ! I'll never get through this mess.

Edward gazed up at the night sky. It had never looked more brilliant and intense. He could see the halo of the Milky Way and the constellations. Yet, in the city, he was surrounded by a darkness that was broken only by cars' headlights and the street lamps.

-I sure hope there's no power outage. If there is, we've had it.

Traffic started moving again.

-About time. Where the hell are the traffic cops?

Once past 57th St., Edward started making good time. Twenty minutes later, he was cruising around Marlena's part of town looking for a parking space. He found one and parked his car in the narrow space; but before getting out, he lit up and reached for the car radio's on switch. The same news: nothing definite, but there was now a new threat of weather disruption. He kept the radio on because the dashboard at least gave off a pale green light.

He rolled open the car window and tapped some of the cigarette ash off the tip of his cigarette. He tried keeping his thoughts methodical, listing his priorities in his mind. What would it all add up to? Maybe nothing; but if the world was gonna' freeze over, he might as well earn his investigator's fee.

Edward tossed his cigarette on to the pavement and this time he got out of his car.

-Why did Marlena pretend not to know me back in April? It's possible she didn't recognize me as an adult, but my name should have rung a bell-

That last though never got finished. The P.I. was struck from behind on the back of the head. Had someone picked up the pavement and flung it in his face? Had someone driven an electrified spike through his head? He lost consciousness before he hit the ground.

CHAPTER FIVE

RADIO BROADCAST. 9 P.M./E.S.T.

"We interrupt all local channels for this emergency broadcast. At approximately 4:00 P.M./E.S.T. the sun vanished from the sky. Astronomers from around the world have not been able to either locate the sun or offer any explanation for its apparent disappearance. Professor Lange of the Hayden Planetarium in New York City cautions that the sun may once again appear in the sky as quickly and mysteriously as it vanished. Professor Lange does confirm that the earth has not moved from its orbit nor have any of the other observed planets and satellites. They remain steady in their respective orbits around a now seemingly empty void in outer space.

"World climate, as of this broadcast, has not yet been affected. However, without the sun's radiation and warmth, temperatures could be expected to plummet at any moment affecting transportation and atmospheric conditions.

"The local police and national guard have been called out and the armed forces are on full alert. All citizens are advised to stay indoors for the time being, unless responding to an emergency. Please stand by for further information."

Susan shook her head.

-Well, that wasn't very reassuring. Yolanda, didn't you mention a Professor Charles Lange once before or was it Dolores who'd spoken about him? I can't seem to remember.

-I attended a couple of his lectures at the Y.M.C.A. Dolores and I- What was that? Someone's at the door.

-I'll get it. You stay here.

-No. Let me go, Susan. It might be Edward. He can take me home.

Marlena shouted after her.

-Be careful. Keep the chain on the door.

Yolanda hurried out into the hallway and opened the front door forgetting to leave the chain on. Edward practically fell on top of her.

-Edward! My God! Are you all right? What happened to you?

-No. And, someone bashed me on the back of the head.

-You're bleeding. Let's get you inside.

Before he knew it, Edward had three females hovering over him. Marlena handed him a shot glass and a silver teaspoon.

-Here. Take these aspirins. I've dissolved them in a spoon for you.

-Thanks, Marlena.

-Were you robbed, dear boy?

-I don't think so.

He reached inside his jacket pocket.

-No. I've still got my wallet…and gun.

Edward downed the whiskey in one gulp.

-And, I'll take another shot of that whiskey, if you don't mind.

-Of course. I'll get you a refill.

He tried sitting up, but the pain in the back of his head didn't make it too easy.

-Yolanda, baby, get that cushion over there? Thanks. Man, my head hurts! It's like an electric current going right down through my spine to my feet.

He leaned his head back.

-That's better. Got a couple of questions for you, Marlena.

-Are you up to asking questions, Edward? Can't it wait?

That was Susan who was trying not to stare at the lump forming on the back of Edward's scalp.

-No. But, I'm going to anyway. Ever hear of a Werner Hoffman? Give it to me straight. Don't play games with me. I need to connect some of the dots.

Marlena handed the P. I. his re-fill and asked her own question.

-Werner Hoffman has come back to America? When was this? Did he bring his son with him?

Edward was satisfied.

-You know him. Good. Yes. He's back, all right. At least the son is back. His father is dead, or so he says.

-I'd nearly forgotten about him. I last saw him and his father some twenty-three years ago in a run down area in Brooklyn. His adopted parents had been killed...probably murdered.

- That "run down area" is working class and it's call Bushwick. What brought you there? You don't exactly fit into that part of town.

-My inquisitive mind? Yes. I'd been attempting to locate the Spear of Longinus. Mr. Hoffman, Sr. also knew of its existence. He would not share his information with me. More fool him. Pompous ass!

Edward knew that Marlena was leaving key points out of her story. Time enough later to get those missing points out of her. Or would there be time? He had to keep probing.

-Why was the boy adopted out? Why did his father come for him on that particular day?

-The biological mother had died and Mr. Hoffman, Sr. was not in a financial position to raise the boy. So I was told.

-Who told you all this?

-A member of Werner Hoffman's Lodge. The man wouldn't give me his name.

-What do you think the real reason was?

Marlena shrugged and poured herself a whiskey.

-To hide the boy until the father could come for him. I'm not sure, but I think that must be the reason.

-Hide the boy for what?

Edward polished off his drink.

-I've no idea. Not really. And, I don't like guessing.

-Have it your way, lady; but, you're holding out on me. Just one more question for now: you know my sister, Nella? You actually met her?

-We met only the one time. I believe she witnessed the adoptive parents' death. Did she never mention this to you, Edward? How strange. Your sister plays her cards close to her chest. I respect that.

-No. And, you never mentioned that you knew who I was those few months ago. Why?

-You were suffering from amnesia. And, we had enough to cope with at the time. And, quite frankly, it didn't seem relevant.

The P. I. got to his feet and almost fell back on to the sofa. He felt the lump on the back of his head.

-Yolanda? You ready to go, baby?

The figure skater put her arm through his.

-Edward, maybe we should stay here for the night. You need to rest. Maybe, we should even call a doctor to have a look at you. You might have a slight concussion.

-No. I'll be fine.

-We can leave tomorrow morning for my place. Look. You can't even stand up.

-In the "morning," baby? Will there be a sunrise tomorrow morning?

PART II

THE DESTROYERS
December 13, 1947

CHAPTER SIX

EDWARD RUBBED the back of his scalp. It hurt real bad, but the couple of aspirin he'd just taken, along with another shot of whiskey, should help. He reached the bottom of the staircase and the smell of bacon made him almost forget the ache in the back of his head and even the nightmare playing outside in the heavens. He looked at his wristwatch: just past 8 A.M.

Yolanda was already up and about when he walked into the kitchen. She was slicing bread and getting the slices ready to put into the toaster. Susan was at the stove frying some eggs and bacon. The P. I. sat down at the kitchen table and looked out the window. Darkness.

-No morning sun, huh? Was the morning paper delivered at least?

Susan answered him.

-No to both questions, I'm afraid. At least, not yet, anyway. One does hope, though.

-Where's Marlena?

-Mother is still asleep. She'll be down later. She was up most of last night in one of her frenzied moods.

-I'll just have some orange juice, Susan. I'm really not that hungry.

Yolanda sat down opposite him at the kitchen table, took his hand and blew him a kiss.

-You have to eat something. When was the last time you ate? I'll bet you had no dinner last night.

-I didn't. Thanks for reminding me, baby. Just maybe I could do with some food.

Susan brought over a plate of bacon and eggs that smelled and looked delicious.

-Man, that smells real good! I just got my appetite back — big time. Suddenly, I'm pretty ravenous.

-I'll get the coffee. Yolanda? Edward? Please, start eating.

Yolanda filled up Edward's plate and, then, helped herself to some bacon.

-Edward?

-What is it, baby?

-Do you have any idea who attacked you last night?

-None. But, they must have been lying in wait for me. God only knows why.

-But, you weren't robbed. They didn't take your wallet or your gun. That makes no sense, just to attack somebody.

Susan brought over the coffee and poured.

-As you know, I make a strong cup of coffee. You might want to put some milk in it. Just a friendly warning. I'll get the sugar bowl.

-Thanks, Susan. And, this bacon is delicious. I'm starting to feel even more ravenous by the second.

-That's a sign of good health.

Yolanda put some cream into her coffee.

-Susan, you should have been a nurse. You're very caring without being annoying.

-No, Yolanda! A doctor, of course. My mother would never approve of my being a mere nurse. Are you joking?

Edward laughed at that. Susan joined them at the table.

-Ladies? Any more news on the radio about our renegade sun?

Susan and Yolanda exchanged looks.

-Don't keep me in suspense even though I'm the sensitive type. Just give it to me straight.

Yolanda took a sip of coffee.

-The astronomers say that everything is as it should be. The stars, the constellations, and even the planets are all in their proper locations.

-So what the hell happened to our sun? It just decided to take a powder? My gut feeling, ladies, is that something or some persons is behind this.

-I wish mother were awake. She might have a few answers or at least some theories. She locked herself in her study, but I could hear her typewriter going.

-Susan, I'd make bet that your mother could at least put forward one theory. But, I don't have time to wait for Sleeping Beauty to get up.

Yolanda and Susan laughed.

-Anyway, I've got a full day ahead of me…of us.

Edward pointed a finger at Yolanda.

-From now on, you and I stick together. Susan? From now on, where your mother goes, so do you. Tell her I said so. It's not safe to wander the streets alone.

Susan put a teaspoon of sugar into her coffee.

-I'll say!

Edward buttered his toast.

-Yesterday, two thugs followed you from the library. Another thug clobbered me on the head. That's no small coincidence. We've been targeted. We stick together in pairs or more. Your mom's house, Susan, will be our unofficial HQ, if that's okay with her.

Susan nodded and helped herself to another slice of bacon.

-I'm sure she wouldn't have it any other way. Oh! The toast is burning!

Susan made a b-line for the toaster.

-Yolanda and I are gonna' shove off in a few minutes. Don't leave the house for any reason and lock the door after us. Savvy?

Susan, holding on to a slice of burnt toast, gave the P. I. a mock salute.

-Yes, sir!

-I'll be in touch throughout the day provided the phones lines are back up.

The three people finished eating their breakfast in silence.

The traffic lights were working and there was a cop on just about every intersection directing the emerging pedestrians and the traffic. Squad cars were everywhere.

Edward tried turning the car's radio on. Nothing but news of the current celestial phenomenon — no big surprise — and most of it speculation or just plain repetition. The scientific community was baffled.

-Yolanda?

-Yes, my darling?

-Did you get a glimpse at Susan's library books: the ones that Marlena sent her for?

-I did. I knew that you'd want to know. So this morning, when Susan was in the kitchen making breakfast for us, I took a look in her briefcase.

-I'm listening.

-One was a book by a Mr. Stuart Russell on the structure and nature of the universe.

Edward slammed his hand down hard on to the steering wheel.

-Oh, brother! Marlena *does* know something. And the other books?

-An astronomy textbook. I think it was some sort of a college textbook, and it looked brand new.

-Um-hmm.

-Why are you smiling like a cheshire cat?

-Any more?

-One book by Professor Werner Heisenberg. Did you know that next to Einstein and Bohr, he's pretty famous? His Uncertainty Principle was the subject of the book. I've heard of him, Edward. His theory states that the more you learn about something, the more you don't know about it.

-Huh? You wanna' run that by me, again?

Yolanda laughed and touched Edward's forearm.

-I know. At first, it doesn't make much sense, but if you think about it, it does. You kind of get an idea of what you don't know.

-Kind of like studying a foreign language. You don't really know the full extent of the vocabulary and grammar,

-Something like that. But, I think he meant it in terms of the physical universe. He was one of the first to put forward quantum physics.

-You're impressing me, Yolanda. Keep it going.

-He went on to say that even by looking at someone or even something inanimate, you somehow affect it...you alter its natural behavior.

-Hmm. So our very existence interferes with everything that it comes into contact with.

-That's a good way of putting it. He even won a Nobel Prize for his work.

Edward mused out loud.

-Did he now? So, if we gaze at the moon, we affect its orbit?

-According to Professor Heisenberg, yes. But, it can't be much of an effect.

-Putting the Professor Heisenberg aside, tell me about your talk with Lt. Donovan.

-You know him?

-The name rings a distant bell. Tell me about him.

-He wants to know who killed Dolores. I think he suspects me.

The P. I. shook his head.

-I doubt it; but, he probably thinks you know more than you're letting on.

-And, he's right. But, I can't let him know that. He'd never believe the truth. Forget it.

-Baby, you can say that, again. I'm gonna' try and pass this car. Hold on.

Edward overtook the car and veered his own car back into the right lane.

-We really don't know who killed Dolores, Edward.

-Don't we? Her murderers are either dead or back in Hell where they belong. It doesn't alter the fact that we're both accessories after the fact. That's a crime, you know.

Yolanda took out her compact.

-Don't remind me. And, this Lt. Donovan seemed pretty intent on solving the case. He was almost passionate about it. It's like he knew Dolores personally.

-Did he?

-No. I'm sure that he didn't. Dolores never mentioned him to me and we talked about everything, especially men.

-That happens a lot, you know. A homicide detective gets caught up in a case and it's almost like a personal vendetta.

He just made the next light, holding to a steady 35 mph.

-Edward, that's not good. It means that he won't give up.

-Not if he's a good detective, he won't. He's probably got some pretty solid scruples. Just stick with your cover story, baby. He's got a dead body and that's all he's got. Nothing more. Which makes me wonder...

-What?

-Dolores' body should have been washed out to sea long ago. What was it still doing in the river?

-Maybe, it sank to the river's bottom and got stuck on something. Gabriel probably weighted it down.

-I guess. But, that's all of eight months ago; it should have been decomposed to practically nothing. Even her I.D. would have disintegrated. Gabriel must have been careless.

-I never thought of Marlena's son as very smart. But, getting back to this nosey Lt. Donovan, won't this emergency keep him occupied? It should. Dolores is dead and no one can help her.

-That's not how our detective sees it and you can make bet on that. From what you tell me, baby, he'll make time for this particular case.

Edward had to slow down for a red light.

-You wanna' light me a cigarette? It's been at least ten minutes since my last one.

Yolanda put away her compact, opened the glove compartment and took out the last pack of Luckies

-Down to my last pack already, huh? I think I'm smoking too much. We'll have to stop off someplace and pick up a carton. I'm back to my old brand.

-Here.

-Thanks.

Yolanda lit one for herself.

-I shouldn't be smoking. My coach would disapprove.

-Just make sure you're not by yourself at any time today. I'll stick around as long as I can at the ice rink; but, I've gotta' pay my sisters a call sometime later.

-I'll go with you. I don't want to be without you. I've been practicing pretty hard the past few weeks and I've got my artistic program down pat. I can skip a couple of days which might even do me some good. Besides, you said that we should stick together.

Edward flashed his girlfriend a smile.

-You won't get an argument out of me. You're my "Girl Friday." Always wanted one.

The young woman snuggled closer to her boyfriend.

-It's cozy in the car with all this darkness surrounding us. And, it feels so warm next to you.

Edward stroked her hair. It smelled very nice.

-You're always cozy. And, I've got a little assignment for you, Miss Friday.

-Oh? Putting me to work already?

-My new client, Mr. Werner Hoffman, Jr. has a few secrets. I tailed him last night to a book shop on 18th right off of 5th. He never said he was going straight home, mind you; but that was the impression he wanted me to have.

-I think that I know that book shop. It's called the The Occult World. I was there a few times with Dolores. They specialize in out-of-print and old books.

-How did she find out about it? And, isn't it funny how Dolores' name keeps popping up?

-Are you being facetious?

-No...not really. It's like she's crying out for justice; that chick just won't stay buried.

-Then, she should rest easy. Her killers are gone.

-I guess. Now, what about this book shop?

-That book shop, Edward, is pretty well known in metaphysical circles. Dolores took me there about a year ago. I went back a few times on my own, but I didn't buy anything. Those books are expensive.

-That's perfect, baby. Then, you won't look so obvious going in there now.

-What am I supposed to do?

-Ask for any books about a Spear of Longinus. Ever hear of it?

Yolanda took a drag on her cigarette.

-I'm not sure. I don't think so. At least, not before you mentioned it last night.

-What's the owner like? Does he run the place or has he got some flunkey running it for him?

-He's the only one I've ever seen there. He's tall and thin with blonde hair. His hair is too long, like a girl's. His name is Wulf and he looks like one, too.

-His last name wouldn't be Holderman?

-I don't know.

-Cozy up to the bastard. Ask him what he thinks about the world's present predicament.

-Do you want me to buy any of his books? There may be a lot of them.

-Get one just to make it look good. I'll put it on company expenses. And, make sure you tell Mr. Wulf that you've got a boyfriend waiting just outside in his car.

-I will.

-One more thing: if you're more than, say, ten minutes, I'll be coming in after you with my gun in hand.

Edward patted the bulge under his suit jacket.

-Do you think I'll be in any danger?

-Maybe. Current events might have Mr. Wulf a little edgy. Just be careful.

-I will.

-And, try to stay near the front of the store. If he tries anything, scream or throw a book through the window. Tell him you're in a hurry and remember: check the guy's reactions.

Edward leaned against the brick wall of the building, just a few feet right of the book shop's display window. He took out a cigarette and lit up. A young woman walked by, glanced at him, and walked quickly away.

-I must've scared her off. Didn't mean to. She wasn't even my type.

He took a deep drag on his cigarette and let out a long puff of smoke.

-I've really gotta' cut down on these; the fingers are starting to turn a little yellow. But, what other vice could I take up at ten cents a pack?

For a few seconds, he held the burning match at eye level. Its flame was like a tiny, bright light in the darkness of the morning. He let the match fall to the pavement: a small but dying flame remained. It went out leaving a blackened piece of compressed cardboard.

-Did our sun just burn itself out? That would mean the end of the world: a slow, cold death. No. I can't believe that. Well...I don't want to believe it. I think our sun is a little more substantial than a burning match. So, where the hell is it?

Yolanda tried not to look back as she entered the book shop. She knew that Edward was standing just outside only a few feet away and this bolstered her courage. The bell over the door's wooden frame announced her arrival. The store was dark and empty, but not at all cold. There was a small checkout counter up front with an antique cash register on it. The two aisles of the store were lined with wall-to-ceiling books.

-Hello. Is anybody here?

She started to walk toward the back of the shop where she knew there was a back room that served as a kitchen and rest area for customers. She stopped short remembering Edward's warning to stay close to the front of the store near the display window.

-Hello? Could someone please help me?

The overhead lights were dim. Yolanda could barely read the titles of the books. She was starting to grow impatient.

-Is there no proprietor about?

She heard movement in the back room.

-Is anyone back there?

A voice called out to her.

-I am the owner of this shop. I will be there in a moment.

Yolanda heard a toilet flushing. In the next moment, a figure of a man approached. He was tall and slender with a pale complexion and long, blonde disheveled hair that fell down to his shoulders. His lips were thin, but his mouth was wide.

-Sorry about the delay. What books would you like to purchase?

His directness and abrupt manner took Yolanda by surprise.

-I'm not sure about the titles.

-Then, what is the subject matter? You surely know that.

-Artifacts: ancient and holy artifacts.

-I see. Are you a collector or an antique dealer? We get a lot of those in here.

-No. It's just an interest.

-How did you come by this "interest" of yours? Don't I know you? You've been here before.

-Only a couple of times.

-With someone else, no? Another girl who was Latin, like yourself. I never forget a face. What is your name?

-What's yours?

-Wulf Holderman. Now, return the favor, please.

Yolanda did not want to give this man her name. She changed the subject.

-Do you have books on ancient artifacts?

-Avoiding my question, eh? What artifact are you interested in? Think you can answer that one? The Ark of the Covenant? The chalice of the Last Supper?

-The Spear of Longinus.

Holderman's face turned to stone. Yolanda would have sworn that it had actually turned grey. He stood there staring her down. The young woman broke the silence.

-What's wrong? You keep staring at me.

-Oh? And, why do you think that is?

Holderman had recovered himself, but the young woman standing in front of him noticed that both his fists were clenched and shaking.

-You are not interested in artifacts, ancient or otherwise. What are you really here for? Tell me at once.

Yolanda took a step back and made ready to leave.

-Stay!

-I'll leave if I want to. You can't keep me here.

-How did you come to know of the spear? Who sent you?

-No one sent me. So, do you have any books on it? You're not such a good salesman.

He screamed out his next sentence.

-Answer me! Who sent you here?

-None of your business. I'm leaving.

Yolanda turned to leave, but Holderman grabbed her by the right arm in a vise-like grip. Now, it was Yolanda's turn to shout.

-My boyfriend's waiting outside. Let me go or I'll start screaming.

-Liar. You're pretty stupid to come here by yourself, you know that?

Yolanda tried freeing herself from his grip. She screamed as loud as she could.

-Edward! Help me! Hurry!

Holderman raised his arm to strike her, but he didn't get a chance to bring his hand down. Edward rushed in kicking open the door. Holderman let go of Yolanda, but this didn't save him. Edward belted him one to the jaw. The store proprietor fell back a few feet but managed to stay upright. Edward didn't give him a chance to recover. He landed another punch right to Holderman's right ear. And, this time, Holderman hit the floor, hard.

-Let's get out of here, baby.

He turned on Holderman.

-And, pal, you're lucky I don't haul you in. Stay healthy, you bastard. I'll be back. You can count on it.

Edward and Yolanda left the book shop and walked to his car.

-Did he hurt you?

-You didn't give him a chance to. My God, Edward! You should have seen his face when I mentioned the spear. It was grotesque. He knows something, that's for sure.

-Tell me all about it in the car.

-Are we going to your mother's house now?

-I want to stop off at my office first. There are some photos I want to show to dear mother and my sister, Nella. Now, let's get the hell out of here.

The ride across the Brooklyn Bridge was taking too long. The traffic was heavy and moving at a snail's pace. Drivers were being careful crossing the bridge and Edward sure couldn't blame them. It was like crossing a bottomless, black chasm: one false step and you were headed straight into the pit of Hell. He and Yolanda had stopped off at his office and picked up the photos of the atomic bomb blasts. They'd also bought some cigarettes and a couple of newspapers. Yolanda was flipping through one of them now.

Edward spoke to his girlfriend, but not about the contents of the newspaper.

-So, his name is Wulf Holderman and Hoffman's father knew him. And, by the looks of it my new client is also acquainted with the Nazi bastard.

-Your new client doesn't have nice friends which doesn't say much for him.

-He sure doesn't. To change the topic: any news on the sun's disappearance in those papers?

-Are you joking? That's all there is practically. It's all theory. No one knows what happened because it happened without any warning. No one could have been prepared for this.

-What about the effects on the climate? Any guesses about that?

-Nothing. I guess the climate hasn't been affected yet.

The P. I. grinned.

-That's the key word, baby, "yet." The media doesn't want to start a panic.

-Traffic's picking up. Is your mother's place far from the bridge? I've never been to that part of town or anywhere in Brooklyn for that matter.

-Not far. It's in Park Slope near the downtown shopping area. It's a red brick house in a row of houses which is suppose to date back about a hundred years.

-I'm a little nervous about meeting your family.

Edward maneuvered the car off the bridge's exit ramp.

-Don't be. Nella's a sweetheart and on the shy side. She's a real book lover, too. Victoria is downright charming. She's the beauty of the family, but don't tell her that.

-Don't you have another sister?

-Two. There's Catrina who everybody hates and not so deep-down-inside. And, then there's Dottie who's the real down-to-earth type. She doesn't live at home because she's a career girl, as she likes to put it. Has her own place out in Bushwick which is the other side of the world. As a matter of fact, it's not that far from where Hoffman's adoptive parents lived and died.

-Did she know them?

-I doubt it. I don't think she was living in that area at the time.

-I'm afraid to ask about your mother.

Edward smiled.

-Dear old Mom? Bedridden for years. She's an invalid who rarely ventures far from her self appointed prison.

-What's wrong with her?

-Beats the hell out of me. Her mind is sure sharp enough. I've always gotten the feeling she's terrified of something or someone.

-What would she be so terrified of?

-Nella and I have asked that question a couple of hundred times.

-And? Any theories?

-Only one: she's terrified of my dead father.

-So, what good will staying in her room do? A closed door can't keep the dead out. I think it must be something else that she's afraid of.

Edward brought the car on to Seventh Ave. And, even in downtown Brooklyn, there were squad cars all over the place. In a couple of minutes, they were pulling into a parking space in front of an old, red brick house. The lights were on and the P. I. could make out his sister's profile through the lace curtains. Good. That meant that Nella would answer the door and put Yolanda at ease. He turned off the car's engine and put his arm about his girlfriend's shoulder.

-Okay, baby, in we go. Ready?

-I guess. Just stay close to me. I hope that they like me.

Edward smiled.

-They will. You're not going in front of a firing squad, you know. Nella and Victoria are very nice. You'll like them. Promise.

-What about your mother and Catrina?

-Let me worry about those two characters.

CHAPTER SEVEN

PROFESSOR CHARLES Lange walked into the East 48th St. building located between 5th and Madison Ave. The book shop on the first floor was closed: a book shop that the professor had initiated and stocked with books of science and technology and philosophy. Books on the theory of quantum physics were there, as this had been an interest of Professor's Lange's and one that had become an ever growing obsession. The theory of a parallel universe existing in tandem with the observable one fascinated him and, for some inexplicable reason, frightened him, as well. Could there be invisible portals bridging the universes? What would happen if such contact occurred? He had to remind himself that it was, after all, just theory.

It was half past 9 A.M. when Professor Lange walked the length of the small, narrow lobby and pressed the elevator button. The doors opened and he pushed the button for the third floor. He held his container of black coffee close to his chest. He liked his coffee black and strong but on the cold side: this "cooling" process gave the coffee its full flavor if it was, in fact, good coffee.

The elevator doors slid open and the professor stepped out into the hallway. His secretary, Mary, was already at her desk. It was she who kept the office in detailed order: files were impeccably kept, bills paid on time, memos typed grammatically perfect and error free, phone calls promptly answered, and messages taken in detail. And, she was the most pleasant woman Professor Lange had ever known. He entered his office.

-Any phone calls this morning, Mary?

-I've got your messages right here, Professor. Mostly reporters asking about the global blackout. That's what they're calling it.

-So, the phone lines *are* back up?

-They sure are.

-I'll be in my office.

Mary handed him the phone messages and Professor Lange looked through them as he walked to his office in the front part of the building.

-What do these reporters expect from me?

He sat down at his desk and rubbed his forehead. He and his secretary had been in his office when the sun had "vanished." After the initial shock had worn off, the two of them had gone over several theories in an attempt to explain the ghastly phenomenon.

"What is it? Please, don't spare me. Do you think your theory about the earth's rotation being affected by A-bomb testing could be the cause?"

"I'd say no, but I wouldn't rule it out. If the Russians have begun A-bomb testing on their side of the globe…"

"Then, it *is* a possibility."

"If that was a question, Mary: then, maybe. But this blackout, for lack of a better term, wouldn't have occurred in an instant and so dramatically."

'Will it last, do you think?"

Mary didn't expect an answer.

"I've no idea. Something inexplicable could be blocking the sun's light from reaching the earth."

"Like what? It would have to be something enormous. That's really frightening."

Professor Lange nodded.

"Yes. It is. It could be a rogue planet that might have entered our solar system undetected. It is a possibility and a most alarming one."

"But, a rogue planet that big? Wouldn't astronomers have seen it?"

"Not if it entered the solar system above the ecliptic plane; but, you're right, it should have been spotted."

"Then, you think this rogue planet might be caught in the gravitational pull of the sun?"

"Maybe, or it could exit our solar system just as quickly as it entered, following its own eccentric orbit. It's just a theory."

Mary hesitated.

"What is it? You're not the shy type. Spit it out."

"Well...it is a pretty wild theory, but could the sun have changed color? I remember your saying once that we see only a small part of the color spectrum."

"Yes."

"Could the sun be giving out a different light...say on the ultraviolet scale? Something that we couldn't see with the human eye?"

"That's not such a wild theory. But, to occur so quickly, in literally the blinking of an eye...that's what is downright frightening. The one theory that I don't dare even think about has to do with a rip in the space-time continuum."

Over the course of the night, Professor Lange had been in touch with Mt. Palomar observatory in California. What they had reported to him was not reassuring: the sun had physically disappeared from the heavens. If the solar globe were truly gone, the Earth's orbit, and every planet's orbit in the solar system, would soon be affected. The elliptical path of the Earth was held in balance by the sun's gravity and without that stabilizing force, the Earth would drift off into interstellar space.

Professor Lange took the lid off his container of coffee, but the black liquid was still too hot for him to drink.

-How in God's name could this have happened? It defies the laws of physics. Where in blazes did the sun disappear to? If it had come to the end of its life's cycle, it would have expanded and we'd all be dead. It would have then contracted into a white dwarf star; but, it would still be in its fixed position in space.

He took a sip of his coffee. Tasted awful. Not worth the wait at the delicatessen or the money. He picked up the phone.

-Mary, would you mind making us a fresh pot of coffee? I think there must be a half a canister left in the cabinet.

-It's already brewing, Professor. I'll bring it right in.

-You're a doll.

Professor Lange sat back in his chair and ran his hand through his thick, grey hair. He tried to control his breathing which would affect his heart. He'd had had some palpitations in the last couple of months and a chronic cough. He'd been cautioned by his physician to take things in his stride and to give up smoking.

-In my stride? My God! With no sun for warmth and radiance, how long can we last? Not too damned long.

He was thinking hard about this when Mary entered his office and put down the cup of coffee on his desk.

-Have you solved the earth's crisis, Professor?

-Not yet. I'd better hurry, though. We may all be living on borrowed time. Was that the phone just now?

Mary nodded and handed the professor her note-pad.

-There were two calls: another reporter form WOR-Radio and a Miss Marlena Lake.

-Marlena Lake? That name rings a bell.

-She was most insistent that you call her back. She said it was a matter of life and death. She had me repeat the message.

Professor Lange laughed.

-Then, I guess we'd better call her back if her life depends on it.

The professor noticed that Mary looked worried. No. Frightened.

-What's wrong?

-Professor, when I opened up the office this morning — I'm sure it was my imagination — I could have sworn that someone left the building just as my back was turned to the door. The air felt so cold, but only for a few moments.

-Cold? The air conditioning certainly wouldn't have been on.

-It wasn't. This cold felt like something from-

-From what?

-From the vacuum of space. It felt like there was no oxygen in the air. I know that makes no sense and I'm sure that it's just my vivid imagination.

Professor Lange's complexion darkened to a grey ash color. He had to take a few deep breaths to recover his composure and maybe an aspirin or two wouldn't be amiss.

-Professor, what is it? You've turned deathly grey. For God's sake-

-Mary, check and see if there's anything missing: start with the files. I'll help you. I don't think you were imagining anything. You get started.

Mary hesitated at the door.

-Professor-

He didn't give her a chance to finish her sentence.

-I've got a few phone calls to make: urgent phone calls. I'll be out shortly. And, Mary, try not to worry. I'll do that for the both of us.

CHAPTER EIGHT

VICTORIA MENDEZ-GONZALEZ was the beauty of the family. Her classic features and gracious manners had endeared her to most people whom she came into contact with.

Victoria had been married briefly to a Mr. Ramon Gonzalez, a stock broker from Mexico City who had emigrated to America. He had lived in the West Village of Manhattan and could be found either at his seat on the stock exchange downtown or browsing through antique stores and book shops. He and Victoria had met at such an antique store near Mr. Gonzalez's residence. Nella had been with her sister at this meeting.

"Victoria? Come and look at this lovely journal."
She walked over to where her sister, Nella, stood.
"It's lovely. I wonder what they're asking for it."

Victoria ran her fingers along the embossed leather binding. Carefully, she opened the blank journal.

"Oh, Nella, even the pages are gorgeous: cream colored and so thick and smooth. I'd be afraid to write in it."

A young man approached the two sisters.

"Don't be." Ramon Gonzalez had startled the two ladies. "Forgive the intrusion. But, this journal should be purchased because a blank ledger is ueselss. I will introduce myself: Ramon Gonzalez. I am a stock broker and fairly new to your country."

The two ladies introduced themselves. Victoria was impressed with him, but her sister, Nella, was not. She didn't trust people who were forward and took liberties.

Mr. Gonzalez continued to speak more and more to the beautiful Victoria, virtually ignoring her younger sister. "The price is not so high on the journal. And, if I may presume? I would like to write a brief note on the first page." Before either Victoria or Nella could respond, Mr. Gonzalez opened the journal, took out a pen from his jacket pocket and began writing. "There. It is done. Don't read it. Here is my business card. Good day."

He walked out of the shop without looking back.

Victoria, against her sister's counsel, contacted Mr. Gonzalez a few days later. To this day, Victoria had never opened the journal. It remained in her dresser wrapped in a silk scarf to this day.

The courtship had been brief and the marriage had ended with Gonzalez's death. He'd been killed In Mexico City under suspicious circumstances. His car had been involved in a head-on collision, but there had been no follow-up investigation by the police. The occupants of the other vehicle had survived the crash and had, in fact, left the scene before the police arrived.

It was difficult and expensive to get his corpse back into the country for burial. Victoria never quite recovered.

-Eddie's told us all about your training for the Olympics. I think it's so exciting you being a figure skater.

-It's a lot of hard work, but it is exciting; especially when you perform well in front of an audience.

-Are you going to the Olympics next year, Yolanda? They haven't been held since 1936 because of the war.

-I hope so, Victoria; but, first I have to qualify in the Nationals. I'd like to go as the National Champion. The international judges would look with favor on that.

-We'll all be rooting for you. I'm sure it'll be broadcast over the radio and maybe even televised. Nella is thinking about a getting a television set for the new year.

Victoria stopped in the hallway and looked up.

-Here we are. I'll just open the trap door and we can go right up on to the roof.

The two women climbed up the wooden ladder. In just a moment, they were standing atop the brick row house and looking up at the new view of the heavens.

-There are so many shooting stars. Look! It's beautiful and kind of scary. It's as if the planet were exposed to both beauty and danger.

-It is exposed. Without the protection of the sun's gravity, the earth could be hit by a meteor at any time. I know that Edward is worried about it. I guess we all are.

-So is our mother. Nella and I have never seen her so terrified.

-Why do you think that is? Edward tells me that she rarely leaves her bedroom.

Yolanda looked admiringly at her boyfriend's beautiful sister. Victoria's complexion was flawless and her honey-colored hair was set in a classic chignon style.

-It's very strange, really. Nobody knows why she's such a recluse, not really.

-When did it start? There has to be a reason.

-It was right after father died. She didn't shed one tear over his death; and, the next day, she started re-arranging furniture and said she would never leave the house under any circumstances.

-What was your father like, Victoria?

-Nice but just a little remote. He was an attorney and preoccupied with his practice. He was always kind to all of us, though, especially Catrina, of course. He was a good provider.

Yolanda smiled at her companion.

-The mysterious sister who is never home.

-And, mother who is *always* home. Interesting, isn't it?

-I wonder if there's a connection.

-I wouldn't be surprised, but you'll never get it out of either one of them. It's as if they're harboring some deep, dark, and mysterious secret. Did I put enough adjectives in there?

They laughed.

-Your sister, Nella, is nice.

-She's got a heart of gold; but, she's too generous and too devoted to dear mother who I'm sure takes advantage of her. Nella could use a good boost in the confidence department, as well. Did you know that she went to college for two years, and she was a straight A student?

-I think Edward mentioned it. What was her major?

-Comparative literature and religion. She always had her nose buried in a textbook; you know, the real thick kind that we mere mortals would never think of reading.

-And, what about your sister, Dottie? I know. I'm asking a lot of questions.

-I don't mind. You're easy to talk to. Always on a diet! She just loves her desserts and her independence. Although...she's not as independent as she makes out. I think she's kind of lonely living on her own. I wouldn't be surprised if she shows up on our doorstep someday soon. It'll be nice to have her back. She's fun.

-So Dottie and Catrina don't live at home.

-Actually, Catrina *does* live at home. She's just never here which is fine with most of us. She's the world traveler thanks to mother's generosity and father's inheritance. But, she doesn't really gain anything by it.

-How do you mean?

-She brings back souvenirs but nothing of the culture and the people she's met. It's all wasted on her. It's like she's just killing time.

-But, killing time for what?

Edward's sister shrugged her shoulders in frustration.

-I've no idea. It's a mystery that Sherlock Holmes couldn't solve.

Edward was sitting in his favorite easy chair in the corner of the living room. It was a room which held so many memories for him: the soft pastel colors of the wallpaper to contrast with the dark, brown pile carpeting. As a boy, he'd sort out his stamp collection with the help of his sister, Nella, who'd always manage to sneak in a foreign stamp. The two end table lamps were lit which gave the room that cozy feeling that Edward use to love so much.

Nella was seated on the sofa right across from her brother. They sat in silence. Nella was nervous and wasn't sure why. In the back of her mind, she felt that she knew the reason for her brother's visit: the sun's disappearance. But, why would he come here for answers? There could be only one reason: mother. Their mysterious and enigmatic mother who guarded her secrets with the tenacity of a rabid dog.

Yes. Her brother had come for information and help. He had also come for a change of clothes. His old room upstairs was always open to him and a couple of his suits still hung in his bedroom closet. He had put on the navy blue suit and a clean white shirt, but no tie.

Edward looked at his sister: the simple, brown dress that she wore, the crucifix that dangled from a gold chain about her neck. His sister who had practically raised him. What secrets had she kept from him? Many.

-Nella?

-Yes, Edward?

They both laughed. Edward felt a little better, but the celestial phenomenon was in the back of his mind. Was it in any way connected to his new client or to his sister? Maybe. In point of fact, he hoped it was.

-A new client came to my office late yesterday afternoon.

-I'm glad. Be sure to get a retainer's fee.

-I did. Thanks. My new client is a Mr. Werner Hoffman. Do you know him?

Nella stopped breathing.

-Nella? You okay? You'd better start breathing, again, or you'll turn a deep shade of blue.

Edward's sister started breathing, again.

-Edward, it's like being hit with a sledgehammer. Werner Hoffman, you say? Was it the father or the son?

-So you do know him. It was the son. He wants me to find something for him: the Spear of Longinus. Know anything about that?

-Yes. I do. I've read about it, but not a great deal has been written about it…very little, in fact. But, Edward-

The P. I. held up his hand.

-One minute. What do you know about this spear?

-It pre-dates mankind. It was planted in the ancient Garden by beings called the Nephilim. Every so often throughout history, this spear reappears and exerts its influence upon mankind and destiny. Adam possessed it. Moses utilized it.

-I'll bet! Who was the last to have it?

-As far as I know, the Roman Centurion who pierced the side of Christ. Actually, he was Longinus

-How did he get a hold of it?

-I've no idea. He may have been part of an Egyptian sect; but, I'm only guessing. Probably, it was one of the spoils of war.

-And, there's been no trace of it since?

-None that I know of, but-

-Go ahead.

-They say that Hitler may have had it or at least one of his cohorts.

-How do you know this?

-I know a few people in occult circles. I attend lectures when I can. It's not often.

-But, Hitler lost the war. I was there, Nella. I fought in that war. So what good did it do the bastard?

-The spear may have been taken from him. Maybe, the spear has a life of its own.

-You mean: no one's saying.

-That's really all I can tell you. I don't know anymore.

-But, you do know Werner Hoffman. Tell me about him.

-It's been over twenty years since I've seen him or his father...and, yet, not a day goes by when I don't think about them. Some events in life, you never forget. They stay with you.

-You witnessed his parents' death.

-No. They were already dead when your sisters and I reached them. They'd been struck down by lightning. Horrible.

-Hoffman said you attended the wake. Why, Nella? Why would you go out of your way to do that? You didn't even know them.

Nella got up and began pacing the floor.

-I'm not sure why. I felt sorry for the boy and...I honestly don't know. Impulse? Curiosity? I felt compelled to go.

-You felt sorry for a young boy whom you only glimpsed in a restaurant? You're too kind-hearted.

-Our mother would agree with you. She would say that I'm too emotional.

Edward took out a cigarette and offered his sister one. She refused.

-Did you meet anyone interesting at the wake?

-You're laughing at me now. There's an ashtray right next to you.

-Thanks. And, I'm laughing at you.

-I did meet someone interesting. She was a rather dreadful woman. I think her name was Marlena Lake. I didn't like her. I can't say why. No. That's not true. She was arrogant and too inquisitive.

-Not too many people do like her. She takes some getting used to.

-You know her, then, Edward?

Nella sat down, again.

-Let's just say that our paths have crossed. But, Nella, when did you start studying the occult sciences?

-You're changing the subject, Edward.

-A P. I.'s privilege.

-At about that time, actually, my interest in the occult was piqued. Does it matter?

-Where did you buy your books?

-In an out-of-the-way book shop on 18th St. I don't know how it stays in business. I've never seen anyone else in there except for the owner.

-This gets better by the second. How'd you find out about this place?

-I'm really not sure.

Edward lit his cigarette. He exhaled some smoke in his sister's direction.

-Come on, sis. This is Edward you're talking to. Give. And, don't let me put words in your mouth.

-Father had spoken about it. He was an occultist, Edward. He belonged to some secret Lodge out in Staten Island. I'm sure mother can tell you far more than I can.

-I'll get to her soon enough. Just one more thing: why were you in that part of town on that particular day?

-It was Dottie's idea.

-Why that day? Why that particular restaurant? What was the reason?

-Just an all-girls' luncheon or so she said. I had my doubts at the time. But, Edward, why does Werner want the spear?

-You two on a first name basis, huh? He didn't say why, not really. He gave some trumped up excuse that he was an art collector.

-That might be true.

-Pull the other one.

-Where is he staying?

-He gave me his card.

He reached into his jacket pocket for the business card that his client had left him. It was gone.

-So, that's what they took. Christ! A friggin' business card.

-What is it?

-I was assaulted last night. Don't fret. I'm okay. Well…almost. My wallet and my gun weren't taken…just that damned business card. Lucky for me I remember the address.

-Where is he staying?

A buzzer sounded and Nella started.

-That's mother. I'll have to get her lunch ready. Would you like to go in and see her?

-I would. And, I'll try not to upset her too much.

The P. I. walked down the narrow hallway to his mother's bedroom. He knocked on the door and went in. The room was well lit and the air smelled of lightly scented roses. Edward also noted that the room was impeccably clean and neat.

-Mother, it's Edward.

-The prodigal son returns. Please come in and sit down. I want to talk to you, young man.

-I'm honored.

-Don't be flippant. You're looking well, but tired. Are things all right with you?

-Until yesterday afternoon, life was just dandy.

The old woman sat upright in bed. She looked at her young son with respect.

-I understand. Edward, what do you make of the sun's disappearance? As a man of the world, you must have some idea. It could mean the end of everything.

-Mother, you don't waste any time. You're the first person in this house to mention our sun's vanishing act. I'm afraid I can't tell you that much. I'm not a scientist.

-From what I've heard, your so-called scientists don't know much themselves. Tell me what you do know. It's vital.

-Astronomers seem to agree on just one fact.

-And what is that?

-Where the sun was, is now only a void in outer space. It's gone.

-But, how is such a thing possible?

Edward's mother sat forward in her bed clutching at the bed sheets. She was agitated and frightened.

-No one seems to know, at least, not yet.

-Why aren't we all dead? How much time do we have left?

-Good questions.

-Edward, come closer to me. You are my only son and there are certain facts that I must share with you.

-Before the world ends, you mean?

-Perhaps, to prevent the world from ending.

Edward took out a cigarette, but didn't light it.

-Mother, does the name Werner Hoffman mean anything to you?

-It does. He was a close associate of your father's. They belonged to the same accursed Lodge. Surprised that I'm telling you all this? And, please, sit down.

-You bet.

-I may have even more surprises in store for you, young man. Your father, Manuel, was head of this Lodge. He was revered and even feared. He was also hated as most talented men are.

-Did this Werner Hoffman hate my father?

-Yes. How did you know his name? Is he still alive?

-His son came to my office late yesterday afternoon. He says that his father is dead.

-The son came to your office? Why?

-He wants me to find the Spear of Longinus.

-Of course! Why else would he come back to America? If he's anything like his father, he's not to be trusted. Did you accept the case?

-You bet.

-Good. Remember: keep you enemies close.

-Did you know that Nella met the Hoffmans years ago?

-She told me something that I already knew. And, she also told me of that evil book shop that she goes to.

Edward shifted uneasily in his chair.

-What is it, Edward?

-Again, that book shop. I've gotta' pay that place another visit.

He told his mother what had transpired earlier that morning.

-I'm not surprised. And, Wulf Holderman is still the owner. He was also a member of your father's Lodge. The last I heard, he had gone back to Germany to join the Nazi movement. A pity he wasn't killed with the rest of them.

-What about the spear, mother? Who had it last?

-Edward, light your cigarette. Who do think had it last?

-I'll bite. Who?

Nella walked into the room carrying a silver serving tray.

-Yes, mother, who did have it last?

She placed the tray on her mother's bed.

-Thank you, Nella. And, you are more versed in the occult than I thought.

Nella sat down in the chair opposite Edward.

-As I just told Edward, the Roman Centurion may have had it last, according to recorded history.

-There is much that is *not* recorded.

-You mean about Hitler's possessing it?

-Yes.

Edward got up and went over to the window. The drapes were drawn and he pushed them aside. It was just a little past noon, but it could have passed for midnight. He took a drag on his cigarette.

-Who actually had it last, mother? I've got a client who's waiting.

-Don't give it to him. And, your sister, Nella, and I have already told you who last possessed it. Even that foul, Nazi creature couldn't hold on to it.

-So why shouldn't I give it to Hoffman?

-He wants to utilize it for some evil purpose. No. Don't smile at me like that, the two of you. I'm not being melodramatic. That spear was never meant to be touched by the uninitiated.

Edward took another drag on his cigarette. He saw that Nella had a question of her own to ask.

-Mother, does that spear have anything to do with the sun's disappearance? You must tell us. We may have very little time.

-I suspect that it does, Nella. I can't be certain, though.

Edward walked over to his mother's bed being careful to point his lighted cigarette away from her.

-Level with us. We've gotta' let go of all our secrets. In a few more days, secrets won't mean too much: they'll be buried under tons of ice.

-Your father was the last of the true initiates to possess the spear. And, like everyone else, he mis-used it. I am the proof of that.

Edward took a drag on his cigarette.

-Where is it now? You know, don't you?

-Nella? Please close the curtains, but first see if anyone is loitering about outside.

123

Nella went over to the window, but could see no one near the house.

-No one is there, mother, only a police car cruising by.

-Close the drapes and join your brother and me.

The ash on Edward's cigarette was about to drop off.

-Is there an ashtray I can use, mother?

-Here. Use this.

She handed her son a porcelain saucer.

-The spear was interred with your father. If the Nazi chancellor lost it — as he surely must have — it should be back in the crypt with your father.

-Mother, that's what you were hinting at before: "Let the dead rest with their secrets."

-Nella! Keep your voice down, for heaven's sake! No one must know this. Men and women throughout the ages have been killed for this spear.

Edward rubbed his chin. He forgot to point his cigarette away from his mother and ended up blowing smoke in her face.

-Yup. You're probably right about that. It's a secret that many have been killed for or worse, I'll bet.

Mrs. Mendez gazed into her teacup.

-There was a rumor that a young woman had gotten a hold of it; this was before I married your father. Her name was Miranda Drake; a beautiful young woman whose family was wealthy. I was to meet with her at Grand Army Plaza, but the meeting never took place. Miss Drake never showed up. The following evening, she was found lying in her bed in a catatonic state. She never recovered.

Edward nodded...almost visualizing the young woman his mother was speaking about.

-I'd like to ask you a couple of dozen questions about that little vignette of yours, mother; but, not now...there's just too much to do and too little damned time.

Mrs. Mendez sat back in her bed, but she was not the least bit tired. Her two children were deep in thought. Edward put his cigarette out in the makeshift ashtray. He was thinking about a mausoleum in Brooklyn...a gravesite near Highland Park. HIs father's burial place. He asked his next question.

-Mother, who put the spear into father's coffin? Was it his Lodge members?

-No. I did.

Nella was stirred out of her reverie.

-You, mother? When was this? Surely, not at the funeral.

-Of course not. A few days later, I and the caretaker placed it in your father's coffin inside the mausoleum.

Edward asked a series of questions.

-What's this caretaker's name?

-A Mr. Milton who knew how to keep his mouth shut. He died not long after. He was a simple and honest man who was well paid for his services.

-How did he die?

-Does it matter? I'm really not sure. I think it was cancer.

-Like yours?

-What are you getting at?

-Who told you to put the spear in with father?

-Why Manuel, himself, of course. It was his final request. It's not something that one puts into a Will.

-And, that's just about the time you became ill?

The old woman gave a deep sigh.

-Yes. It was never intended that I should hold that sacred object.

Edward grinned.

-Some "sacred" object. This thing sounds pretty dangerous. Is it radioactive? Sounds like it.

-It emits a form of energy. I don't know what it is. No one does.

Edward took out another cigarette.

-Okay. So, we know where the spear *should* be assuming that no one has helped himself to it and that it did, in fact, do a return trip to my father.

He burst out laughing.

-How many assumptions did that add up to?

-Edward, you must go there at once.

The P. I. shook his head.

-We'll keep the lid on this for now, mother.

-Why would you wait? I think it's vital that we have it in our possession.

Edward laughed.

-You can't wait to get your hands on it, huh?

-You're wrong. It is *you* who must handle it. No one else. You are an initiate even though you are not aware of it.

Edward chose to ignore the last part of his mother's statement.

-What exactly can this spear do?

-It can shatter worlds.

-And, make stars disappear?

Mrs. Mendez leaned forward as if she'd just had a revelation.

-It's possible. Yes. We must assume that.

-Who would know for sure?

-Your new client, Werner Hoffman, would be privy to such knowledge. His father might have confided in his son. He must have. And, there was a Frenchwoman who was also involved.

-Hoffman mentioned her. Anyone else?

-There was a Mr. Ricardo Montenegro. He may still reside in New York City. I've lost touch with his other Lodge members: hangers-on, most of them. They had no use for me.

Edward grew a little impatient with his mother.

-Mother, who was father's confidante, besides yourself? Every leader has to have a second-in-command; a successor, if you would

It was now Mrs. Mendez's turn to be impatient with her young son.

-Why do you want to know, Edward? There was no successor, as far as I know; there should have been, but there wasn't And, besides, we know where the spear is. What else is there to know? We've no time to go tracking people down.

-We might be assuming a lot. The spear may not be in the crypt.

The old woman was pensive for a moment.

-I know of no other members who can be contacted. It was a secret Lodge. They trusted no one, especially women.

-That makes sense. But, if you can think of anyone else-

-Confide in no one, Edward. You also, Nella. This knowledge puts all of our lives in danger.

-My gut instinct tells me to wait just a couple of days. I need to get a few more pieces of this puzzle together.

Nella took her mother's tray off the bed.

-You're tired, mother. Lie back and I'll get your medicine.

-I am not tired. If nature is not put to right, we're all doomed.

-Were there any women in this Lodge?

-No. That frenchwoman fancied that she was, but she wasn't. Why do you ask?

The P. I. laughed.

-I know one woman who'd give her right arm to have been a member. Surprised she wasn't.

-Are you referring to me, young man?

-No. Not you, mother. Although, you did cross my mind.

-Well, Edward, how did your meeting go with your mother and sister? You've been quiet ever since we left your house, you know. Cat got your tongue?

Yolanda was not to be put off by her boyfriend's silence.

-Do you know that you left those photographs that you took from your office in the glove compartment?

-I know. And, I found out a lot more than I thought I would. It's kind of a maelstrom in my head right now.

-You going to tell Yolanda about this storm?

Edward turned the car on to Seventh Avenue and headed uptown. He filled his girlfriend in on all the details, even though some of it might be dangerous for her to know. He reasoned that all their lives were in danger anyway. Yolanda was resourceful in her own way and she just might throw some light on to things.

-Your mother knows a lot. I wonder if she told you everything, her type usually doesn't.

-You haven't even met her yet; but, you've sized her up pretty good. Any thoughts, baby?

-This Lodge of your father's sounds creepy.

-It hit me like that, too.

-What was their purpose for existence: to be wealthy, powerful, influential?

-Beats the hell out of me, but I'd say all of the above.

-Where is it? I'll bet that she didn't tell you.

Edward stopped the car for a red light and lit the cigarette dangling from his mouth.

-She didn't. I didn't ask. I should have. I knew you'd come in handy.

He leaned to his right and kissed his girlfriend square on the mouth. He released her and stepped on the gas. Yolanda had a few more questions for him.

-How does all this information help us? What does it tell us about the sun's disappearance? Is there any connection, Edward?

-In a couple of well chosen words, baby: I don't know. But, if there's the slightest chance of a connection, we've gotta' follow it through because there's nothing else we can do and it sure beats doing nothing.

-Are we headed back to Marlena's place?

-No. What I want to do is drop you off at the ice rink. Don't worry, I'll be staying with you. You know that maelstrom I was just talking about? Well, I gotta' calm it down and try and make sense out of these last twenty-four hours. We'll see Marlena tonight.

-I'm glad. I was feeling guilty about missing a training session. I'm sure that my coach is there.

-And, tomorrow, I wanna' pay my new client a visit and shake him down.

-Edward? Don't tell him about your father or the mausoleum. He could be involved with dangerous people like that awful Wulf at the book shop or the people who followed Susan. I'll just bet that he is. You saw Hoffman go in Wulf's book shop, didn't you? You don't go into that book shop for no reason.

-He was holding out on me and I want to know why. We don't have time for cat and mouse games.

CHAPTER NINE

EARLIER THAT day, there had been a disturbance in Professor Charles Lange's office. Marlena Lake had pushed her way past the Professor's secretary and barged into his private office unannounced.

-I'm sorry Professor, but there was no stopping her. She brushed right past me.

-It's all right, Mary.

Mary turned to leave, but before closing the door behind her, she gave Miss Lake her most disapproving look.

-Please, sit down, Miss Lake.

Professor Lange's visitor was already seated and making herself comfortable.

-Nice office you've got here. Business must be booming.

-Was that a statement and a disparaging one at that, Miss Lake?

-A pointed observation. I take in things and people.

-Go on, please.

-I'm here for information and I expect you to come clean. I'm not the sensitive type. And, I don't scare easily.

-Who are you? And, how do you know about me?

-A girlfriend of mine attended one of your lectures at the Y. I was impressed with what she had to say. Now, as to your first question, I'm a practitioner of the occult sciences like yourself. And, don't waste my time in trying to deny it.

-How can I help you?

-How long do we have? Don't mince words, just spit it out. I must know.

-The planet will be frozen solid within two months.

-But, we'll all be dead before then.

-Yes. The human race might have three weeks…maybe a little more but not much. Within the next ten days, outside transportation will be next to impossible. Global blizzards will sweep across the planet and the essential food chain will be disrupted resulting in worldwide famine and-

Professor Lange hesitated.

-Go on.

-The planet might drift off its orbital course into deep space; and even the Earth's rotation will be affected.

Marlena sat back in her chair and loosened the silk scarf about her neck.

-Not a pretty picture, is it, Professor?

Professor Lange smiled with grim satisfaction at his unwelcome guest.

-A doomsday scenario, Miss Lake. You didn't want it sugar-coated.

-Which means that something must be done within the next ten days while we're still able to move about.

-Better play it safe and make that one week. The temperatures across the globe will start dropping soon.

-What's keeping the earth warm now?

-The earth has a rotating molten core which radiates thermal heat and that is why we haven't frozen to death yet. It can't last much longer. It needs the sun's radiant energy to keep it in place and to restore the core's output of energy. That critical balance has been upset, perhaps irrevocably.

Marlena leaned forward in her chair.

-What exactly has happened to the sun? Where the hell is it? Did it collapse into nothing?

-I don't know

-Liar. I demand an answer. A star cannot simply vanish: there's trickery involved here. I warned you before to come clean, Professor Lange. I don't make idle threats.

-I don't like being threatened-

Professor Lange didn't get a chance to finish his sentence. Marlena had taken her pistol out of her pocketbook and was pointing it straight at his forehead.

-I carry through with my threats. Now...I want to know what you know about the sun's so-called disappearing act. Who is responsible and how and why was it done?

-You give me more credit than I deserve. I can't be sure.

-Then, *guess*. And, make it good or this gun goes off and the top part of your head with it.

-As a scientist, I can't offer you any answers.

-And, as an occultist, Professor Lange? I'm getting impatient.

-The sun could have shifted to...

-Go on. Where? Tell me!

-It could have shifted to another dimension through a rip in the space-time continuum.

-What the hell does that mean? Another dimension or a parallel universe? That's nothing but theory just like your so-called quantum mechanics.

-Miss Lake, it's difficult to think with that gun pointing at me.

-Too bad. How and why was the sun "shifted?"

-So that the earth would freeze over.

-Who would want such a thing to happen: only a madman.

Something clicked in Marlena's head. She lowered the gun, but held on to it.

-Professor, during the last war, the Nazi's had sent expeditions down to the Antarctic. Do you know what they were looking for?

-Yes.

-What?

-An ancient race that even pre-dates the Sumerians: the Anunnaki: beings from another world, or so the legend goes.

-Yes. I've heard of that theory: beings from the distant past who may actually have colonized the Earth. During the last great axis shift, the continent of Antarctica found itself frozen at the bottom of the world: that is where this race is said to have established one of its cities.

Professor Lange picked up the story.

-The earth's axis had shifted, Miss Lake, at least, that's the theory. The result was cataclysmic. I believe it is they who may have shifted the sun, but nature has a way of correcting itself. If the survivors of this race or the Nazis, themselves, are responsible, it would take a great deal of energy to execute such a thing and the same amount of energy to maintain the shift. They may not have that energy available to them. The sun could shift back to its original position in space.

-But, we can't just wait for that to happen, Professor. It may be too late by then assuming that it does reverse itself. And, by the way, what Lodge did you belong to?

-I was waiting for you to ask that. My Lodge was located near the ocean in Staten Island and it had no name.

-Give me its exact location.

-Near South Beach right off of Oak Terrace.

-Good. I'm not unfamiliar with that district.

-You're not thinking of going out there? If there are any members still about, Miss Lake, they'll kill you.

-*Are* there any members still about?

-The Lodge disbanded after our leader's death. I've never gone back.

-You sound frightened. Why?

-I was a fool to have been persuaded to join. I was young and ambitious.

-I must leave you now, Professor. My daughter is waiting for me downstairs. And, as I've told you: I don't frighten easily. Thanks for the information.

-You're welcome, Miss Lake.

-Good day.

Marlena put her gun back in her pocketbook and left. She walked past Mary's reception desk and buzzed for the elevator. The doors slid open and she stepped inside. Her mind was buzzing with thoughts.

-Sumer? That ancient city…that virtually unknown culture that was so advanced…it was mentioned somewhere…someone mentioned it. There was a reference to it somewhere on paper.

She couldn't bring the exact moment or place to mind: a loose end that would have to wait.

PART III

NIGHT GAMES
December 14, 1947

CHAPTER TEN

EDWARD AND Yolanda were driving past Columbus Circle and heading toward 72nd St. It was early evening.

-We're almost there. Hold up! What the hell's going on?

Right at the corner there was an ambulance and a squad car parked in front of an apartment building. The entrance to the apartment house was cordoned off and two police officers were holding back the small crowd of curious onlookers. Edward made an illegal U-turn and parked right in back of the squad car.

-That's the building where Hoffman lives. I wonder what's going on.

-I hope that nothing's happened to him. I don't see anyone in the ambulance.

-Not yet, anyway. I'm going on up, baby. Stay put and don't leave the car. Keep all the doors locked and don't let anyone in except me.

He was about to climb out of the vehicle when Yolanda grabbed him by the arm.

-Edward, look! They're taking something out of the building.

-What the hell is it?

-Look how they're carrying it out. It looks heavy. They're straining with it.

It took four men to carry out the stretcher and whatever was on it was covered with a black tarpaulin. The attendants heaved the thing into the ambulance and each man had to catch his breath. Two of the attendants climbed into the ambulance with the stretcher while the other two slammed the double doors shut. Those two men went around to the front and the ambulance started off.

-They must be headed for Roosevelt Hospital. I'll be as fast as I can. Remember: no one gets in this jalopy but me. You should be all right with that squad car parked right in front of you. Any emergency, just honk the horn 'till I come a running.

Edward got out and slammed the car door shut. He heard Yolanda click the door locks shut. Good. He walked over to and ducked under the police barricade. He showed his I.D. to one of the patrol cops and was let through.

He entered the building. It was old New York but well maintained. Edward's footsteps resounded on the terratza floor as he walked by framed photos of its famous inhabitants both present and past. He made a left at the end of the hallway and walked toward the first of two elevators. He opened the door of the first elevator and pressed the button for the fourth floor. When he got off, the apartment door directly ahead was open. People were moving about: it was the forensics team. Had that been Hoffman being carried out?

The apartment was in a shambles: furniture over-turned and ripped apart, floorboards forced open and broken glass was all over the place. Without being aware of it, he turned his coat collar up to keep out the chill. He took a few steps into what had been Werner Hoffman's living room. Even the curtains and blinds had been ripped down and then ripped apart.

A man approached him. He was tall and blonde and about forty. His voice was deep and gravelly, but clear.

-Can I help you, pal? You just walked into a crime scene.

-Edward Mendez, P. I.

-You a friend of the former occupant?

-No. He was a client of mine. I take it that we're talking about Mr. Werner Hoffman, Jr.?

-Your client's been murdered. You might have passed the stretcher in the hallway just now. You must have.

Edward was incredulous.

-That was Hoffman? I don't get it.

-You told me your name. I'll tell you mine: Lt. William Donovan. You've got a girlfriend by the name of Yolanda Estravades who I met the other day.

-She mentioned it. As a matter of fact, she's waiting for me outside. But, let's get back to Hoffman. How was he killed?

-I'll get to that detail in a second. What brings you here at this time of night? Christ! It's eternal night.

-That's why I'm here.

-Come again?

-I met Werner Hoffman for the first time late yesterday afternoon. He wanted me to find something for him.

-Like what?

-I'm not at liberty to say.

-Hey, pal, he's dead…real dead.

-How was he killed?

-Not sure. But, the neighbors heard what sounded like some kind of war up here. They called the cops. When we arrived-

-What?

Lt. Donovan shook his head and put away his notepad.

-The squad came across this block of blue ice. One of them touched it and just about got his fingers frozen off. They could make out the body of a man inside: it was Hoffman…frozen alive. I'd never seen anything like it. His eyes and mouth were wide open like he died of fright first.

-Would you mind if I walked over to the window? I want to check on my girlfriend.

-Go ahead. But, those squad cars aren't going anywhere. She oughta' be safe enough.

Edward walked over to the window. His car was parked where he'd left it and that was Yolanda sitting in the front passenger seat. He turned back to the lieutenant.

-Good. Are you gonna' do an autopsy on Hoffman?

-You bet. First, we need to get that ice off of him and that's not gonna' be easy. We had to get ice tongs to get it on to the damned stretcher. It took four attendants to lift the damned thing and carry it downstairs.

Edward. took out a cigarette and lit up. He offered one to Lt. Donovan who refused.

-Level with me, Mendez: what do you make of all this? It's like something out of a Universal horror movie: this and the sun's disappearance. Is there some kind of a connection?

Edward smiled ruefully.

-You sound like me, Lieutenant. I'm hoping there is. I'll rephrase that: I'm *praying* that there is.

-What did Hoffman want you to find?

-A spear.

-Say what?

-An ancient spear that pierced the side of Christ.

-You gotta' be kidding me. What the hell for?

-I don't know.

-Got any idea where it is? Can it help us out? And, what the *hell* am I saying?

-Yes to the first question. Don't know about the second.

-My men are finishing up here. Let's head downstairs. We can use the stairwell. I want to talk to you.

Lt. Donovan checked with his forensics team and then joined Edward who was waiting for him just outside the apartment.

-Let's head on down. And, pal, tell me all you know 'cause we don't have much time left. We've been getting radio bulletins at the precinct all day and they ain't been too pleasant.

-Do I want to hear this?

-Nobody *wants* to hear it. The sun is gone and all that's left is a friggin' void where it oughta' be. And, that's not the worst. Scientists expect the temperature to start dropping real soon and fast. We might have only days left.

-I'll come clean with you, Lieutenant, but let's get outside first. Man, it was freezing in that apartment!

Edward and Lt. Donovan stepped outside on to the sidewalk. The two patrol officers were still on duty. The police lieutenant took a good look around the area, gazing skyward for just a second.

-You see these tall buildings...all these skyscrapers here in the city? If the sun doesn't come back, the atmosphere is gonna' turn to solid ice. We'll all be buried under millions of tons of the stuff. It'll crush everything on the surface of this damned planet of ours: the skyscrapers will be shifted and leveled like wet cardboard.

He took a deep breath.

-So, Mendez, if that spear-

Edward interrupted.

-Cigarette, Detective?

This time, he accepted.

-Thanks.

-Thought you might need one.

The two men waved to Yolanda sitting in the car.

-You know, Mendez, I can take murder, robbery and just about anything you can come up with except-

Lt. Donovan pointed at the night sky: the Milky Way was like a lattice of crystal strung against the blackness of outer space.

-that! Where the fuck is the sun? How does a star just blink out in an instant? How? *How*? The big-wig scientists say that it defies all the natural laws of physics.

And a light went off in Edward Mendez's head.

-My God! Lieutenant, you just might have said the key word: "natural." You hit the nail on the goddamned head!

Edward threw down his cigarette. It hit the pavement like a red and white glowing asteroid.

-That's it! It's not natural. How the hell *could* it be? The spear *is* the key to all of this. Whoever killed Hoffman thought the poor bastard had it. There's got to be a connection between the sun's disappearance and the spear.

-You'd better be right. They're giving us ten days at best before the weather cripples transportation.

-Does that include today? I'm not joking with you.

-It does. And, Mendez, I've gotta' get down to Roosevelt for that autopsy. You got a card you can give me?

He and the police detective exchanged business cards.

-We gotta' get moving on this. For now, I'll put the Sarney case on the back burner.

Edward took out another cigarette.

-You can extinguish it. Neither I nor my girlfriend know anything about how Miss Sarney was murdered and that's the bonafide truth.

-Tell me the whole truth, pal, because I've been in this business too long. Your girlfriend's real pretty, but-

-I'm not lying to you. Yolanda and Dolores were best friends and confidantes. But, if it makes you feel any better, put it on that ole' back burner.

CHAPTER ELEVEN

EDWARD FINISHED talking to Lt. Donovan. The two men agreed to meet the next day at Police HQ on the upper east side and compare notes. It had been a long and trying day for both of them and they were tired and hungry and on edge. It wouldn't take much to set either man off.

The P. I. jumped into the driver's seat of his car and locked the door. Yolanda was full of questions.

-So, what was it that the attendants were carrying out? Not Mr. Hoffman. It couldn't be. Was he a heavy set man?

-It was Hoffman, all right, in a block of ice. He was murdered: terrified and frozen into the bargain.

It took Yolanda a couple of seconds to digest this news, but what she finally said was interesting.

-Like all of us will be if the sun can't be brought back.

-You're right, baby. And, that spear is the key to it all.

-Edward, we have to get it and fast. We've already wasted too much time.

-That might be dangerous and it might not be where we hope it is.

-I think it's worth the risk, don't you? We really don't have any choice. There's nothing else we can do.

-I wish I knew what the hell it was. It kills people or incapacitates them. Look at my mother. It killed my father, probably, and that caretaker. And, if Hitler had it, would it somehow get back to my father?

-Why not? It's no ordinary spear. It might be some sort of advanced mechanism that we don't understand.

-You're sharp, baby. What's magic to us may be common place science to another civilization.

-Like the Sumerians. No one really knows that much about them: where they originated from and how advanced they were.

Edward turned over the engine and pulled out of his parking space.

-Right now, I need to eat and so do you.

-There's an automat nearby on 61st St. We can go there and it shouldn't be too crowded. The food's pretty good for what you pay.

-And, that's close to Roosevelt Hospital. I'd like to know the results of that autopsy they're doing on Hoffman. It might tell us something.

-Who do you think could have killed Mr. Hoffman?

-Beats me. There's- what the hell's going on?

A black van had driven alongside Edward's car and was forcing him over to the curb, almost scraping against the P. I.'s car.

-Edward! He's forcing us off the road.

-Playing "chicken," huh? Bastard. I'll fix him.

Edward speeded up and ran a red light, but so did the black van.

-We've got a lead on the creep. I'm gonna' make a sharp left and head down Central Park. Hold on tight, baby.

The P. I. floored the gas pedal and made a sharp left hand turn down 63rd St, headed toward the park and, then, made a sharp right.

-As soon as we hit Columbus Circle, I'm gonna' park and we'll head to the nearest subway entrance.

-Why the subway?

-That van looks like it's metal plated. It can wreck this car and us in it. If they wanna' follow us on foot, they'll be forced to show themselves. Just get ready to run.

-Maybe, we should try to make it to the Third Ave. El?

-No chance, the elevated lines might not be running. We'll stand a better chance underground.

He drove down Central Park West like a maniac, ran a couple of red lights, and spotted a parking space right on 59th St.

-Edward, that van is still following us.

What Yolanda saw next terrified her.

-Oh, my God! They just ran the intersection and ran over a cop. Edward, they must have killed him…crushed him to death.

-Why the hell am I not surprised? Bunch of murdering pricks! I'm gonna' park right about *here*! Grab your purse, roll up your window, and lock the door from the inside.

Yolanda grabbed her shoulder bag.

-I'm ready.

Edward practically slammed into the parking space, not a neat fit, but the cops wouldn't be handing out any tickets. In half a second, they were out and running along Columbus Circle and heading for the nearest subway entrance.

-Over there, Edward! We can ride the A train down to 42nd, there's a connecting crosstown tunnel to the shuttle at Times Square.

-Good girl. Come on.

Yolanda glanced over her shoulder.

-That van- I think it spotted us.

The black van had slowed down and was looking for them. The beam of a powerful flashlight shone from the passenger side. The few pedestrians about were startled by the flashlight's brilliance: it wasn't missing a single face in the crowd, and it was fast approaching Edward and Yolanda.

-Run, baby! That beam's catching up to us.

In another second, they were on the top step of the subway entrance when the flashlight's beam struck Edward full in the face.

-Rotten bastards!

They ran down the stairs and along the narrow tunnel that lead to the token booth. The train was just pulling into the station.

-No time to buy tokens. We'll just take a free pass on this ride.

They ducked under the wooden turnstiles and made straight for the train that was just slowing down.

-Oh, my God! It's taking it's time pulling in. Edward-

The P. I. grabbed her by the arm and propelled her forward along the platform's edge.

-Let's move up further just in case our friends are heading in our direction.

They moved up a few yards as the train came to a halt and the doors slid open. The two of them got in, but stayed close to the doors keeping an eye out for any late arriving commuters. The doors stayed open.

Yolanda was on the verge of screaming.

-Why don't they close them? What are they waiting for?

-Take it easy.

The P. I. looked down the train platform. Maybe a red light was holding the train up or there was a sick passenger or the weather outside could be affecting the rails. The seconds ticked by real slow.

At last, the doors slid closed.

-Edward, I saw a man and a woman get in.

-Could you make them out? Did you notice anything about their features?

-The man was tall and the woman looked middle-aged. I couldn't see their faces too good.

The train pulled out of the station. It was a down-town train. Edward leaned against the door.

-I think it's just two stops to 42nd.

-There should be more people around, it's a major terminal. We should be safer.

-Don't bank on it. They were after Susan on 5th Ave. in broad daylight. These killers don't care about witnesses.

-Trying to make me feel better? Look. We're pulling into 50th St,

The train stopped and the doors slid open. No one got into their car.

-Good. We're almost there, baby.

Edward kept an eye on the connecting doors of the train, half expecting the couple that Yolanda had spotted to come charging in. He moved away from the door to get a better view of the car behind them. He spotted their pursuers in that next car. They were moving toward the connecting doors.

Yolanda grabbed her boyfriend's arm.

-That looks like the woman Susan described. She's middle-aged but-

-But walks like a man.

-Edward, they're coming this way.

-Let's not wait for them. Come on!

The young couple made for the next car. As they were opening the connecting door, their pursuers entered the car.

-Hurry, baby.

He pulled Yolanda through the doorway and slammed the door shut behind them. They were now riding between cars. Yolanda pulled at the sliding door to get into the next subway car, but it wouldn't budge.

-Edward, I can't open it. It's stuck.

-Let me have a try. Careful! You almost fell through the gap.

He yanked at the handle, but the door wouldn't slide open. He glanced back. Their pursuers were only a few feet away.

-Edward, try the latch on top. Maybe, that will open it.

The P. I. jiggled the latch. It worked. He yanked the car door open as the train entered the terminal at 42nd St. The young couple got into the next subway car and this time Edward jammed the latch on top to lock the connecting door in place.

The train came to a halt. Their pursuers were pulling at the jammed door, but couldn't get it open. The conductor opened the train doors and Edward and Yolanda ran out on to the station platform and up the nearest stairwell. When they reached the upper platform, they looked frantically around for the connecting crosstown tunnel. Yolanda spotted it.

-Edward, it's over there.

They ran down the platform, dodging fellow commuters.

Edward almost laughed out loud.

-Talk about into the breach.

They slowed down to a fast walk to catch their breath. Edward turned around to see if they were still being pursued. They were.

-Pick up the pace, baby. We've got company behind us and it ain't friendly.

-Where's your gun?

He tapped his left upper chest.

-Right here. And, it's loaded.

-Good. I think you should use it.

-They haven't attacked us yet. It wouldn't be self defense. But, if I have to, I'll shoot to kill. Count on it.

Edward and Yolanda were running again. Their pursuers were now openly chasing them. All pretense was gone. The P. I. and his girlfriend were about a third of the way down the tunnel and their pursuers were gaining on them.

-Christ! For an old bag, she's running like a friggin' track star.

-Edward, she's not old. It's some kind of disguise. Get ready to shoot. Please!

-You get ready and just keep running. I'm gonna' try to slow those two creeps down.

He got his gun out of its shoulder holster. He turned around, crouched down to get leverage, and took aim at the oncoming male pursuer. A woman commuter saw this, dropped her purse, and screamed.

The P. I. fired and hit the man in the chest. This slowed him down, but didn't stop him. His female companion grabbed her cohort by the arm. He recovered, but by this time, Edward had caught up to Yolanda and the two of them headed for the Times Square shuttle train that was getting ready to leave. They ran down the last few yards of the tunnel and shoved past commuters. Just in time, they leaped into the last subway car as the doors slid closed. The train pulled out and as it did, something smashed against the car window. It was the woman pursuer pounding her fist, trying to break the glass. It cracked, but didn't shatter.

The train pulled out of the station.

-That was a close one. But, at least this time, we left those two jokers behind.

Yolanda was still gasping for air.

-Edward, will we be any safer at Marlena's?

-Probably not. But, that townhouse of hers is built like a damned fortress: steel frames on all the doors and bars on every window. We should be safe enough if we can reach it.

-Who are they? Why are they after us? Why do they want to kill us?

-We're some kind of a threat to them and their plans, baby. We know too damned much and they — whoever "they" are — can't take any chances.

-What about Mr. Hoffman? Did they think that he knew where the spear is? Then, why kill him?

-I don't think he knew where it was. He hired me for that. Remember? But, he did know my sister, Nella.

-Then, she's in danger, too.

-I've been worrying about her. I know the police chief in their precinct so as soon as we get to Marlena's, I'll have them post a squad car outside the house.

-Better do it as soon as we get there. I like your sisters.

In another few minutes, they were riding uptown on the Lexington Ave. local. They got off at 86th St. with a few other non-threatening commuters. The P. I. and his girlfriend hailed a taxi to take them crosstown to Marlena's place.

CHAPTER TWELVE

ANGEL ULYSSES CORREA sat on his stoop in the Bushwick section of Brooklyn. It was three o'clock in the morning and the streets were deserted and there was no traffic coming down the narrow one way street. The local bus had stopped running at about midnight. The nineteen year old looked up at the magnificent night sky. He didn't like what he saw. He yearend for the return of the sun: the warmth and brilliance of the solar globe.

Angel was no longer human. He had been transformed into something unnatural and predatory. He was still a handsome young man: an amateur body-builder, in fact, with a chiseled physique. And, now, at this moment, he felt cold…too cold. He needed the vital nourishment of the sun's rays. He'd settle for human blood. An outcast, this would be the last time he'd see his old neighborhood in the lower-middle class section of the borough. He was an immortal. He needed a victim and he wasn't choosey about whom he selected.

-So, what in Christ's name happened to the sun? Is this God's revenge on me? My immortality was forced on me. You hear that? My rotten girlfriend tricked me into going into that funeral parlor. Her and her conniving friends are gonna' have to pay for what they did. But, that's gotta' wait until I can get them…one by one.

Angel stared up at the street lamp for no particular reason other than the fact that it gave off light. He didn't hear the man approaching him. If he had, he might have attacked him. He'd been taught the art of the kill by the mortician who had transformed him and now he had to put it into practice. He glanced up at the second story window in his apartment building. What was she doing up at this hour? What the hell was her name?

Dottie Mendez had not slept that night. It was close to three o'clock in the morning, too late to even think of trying to get some sleep. She got off the couch in her living room and went in search of a cigarette. She needed to do something…anything to occupy the last few hours before she could decently get dressed and go to work.

On her dresser bureau, there was the newspaper. She flipped through the pages of "The Night Owl" edition of the Daily News. Depressing. Amazing all the coverage that was given to a hole in outer space. And, what in the name of heaven and hell did all this speculation amount to? Nothing.

She turned to the sport's section: the ice hockey game had been cancelled at Madison Square Garden; as a matter of fact, all upcoming events had been cancelled. She enjoyed going to the Garden and mixing with the crowds of people who wanted to forget their troubles for a brief time. Dottie was the social type and would talk to anyone who happened to be sitting next to her or even a few chairs over. It also helped that she was a sports enthusiast and could out shout most fans. And, once you started on those hot dogs, you were dead!

She threw the paper down in disgust and, once again, got up off the couch.

Dottie had been thinking of her late father: Manuel Mendez. Would he know what had caused the sun to do a vanishing act? She knew that he had been an occultist. He hadn't told her; but, she had the habit of listening in at keyholes. And, her favorite keyhole was her parents' bedroom. Her mother had done most of the talking, but her father had provided a few key answers; not enough to be sure, but just enough information to whet his daughter's appetite for the occult sciences; just enough to tell her that there was more to life than the mundane.

Her elder sister, Catrina, had always been privy to her parents' confidences. Why her mother and father should favor this shallow and self-centered creature was beyond Dottie's comprehension; her too thin sister with her Paris make-up and clothes that were not at all flattering. Why had her parents pampered her so; because she was basically a moron who pretended to be an intellectual?

Dottie walked into her bedroom which looked out on to the street. On the end table next to her bed was a pack of cigarettes. Thank God. She took one out and lit up. She smoked too much just like her kid brother, Eddie. Her doctor had warned her to cut back, but a cigarette helped kill her appetite for too many sweets. It was worth the risk of lung cancer even though she already suffered from bronchitis.

It was too cold to open up the window, but she did gaze down at the sidewalk below. Wasn't that Angel out there? What was he doing out so late? Wasn't he usually tucked away in bed at this ungodly hour? He was pretty rigid with his comings and goings. A real muscleman...too bad he was so young and unapproachable. Why was he staring up at the lamp post like that?

A man coming down the street caught her attention. This man approached Angel and began talking to him. The young boy looked almost frightened of the man; but, he recovered quickly enough. The conversation was brief. The man left in the direction that he had come in. Dottie tried to get a good look at his face, but his fedora was pulled too far down. It looked as if the man's face was burned...but that had to be her imagination. It was probably the effect of shadow and light. She turned away from the window, but too late. Angel had spotted her.

Angel watched the man walk up the deserted block and disappear into the night. What the man had said to him, he put out of his mind…for now. It was time to get some sleep. He turned around to go inside but once again looked up at the second story apartment window. That old busybody was still staring out her window. She was smoking and Angel could make out her face by the light of the cigarette and the lamp. He went inside and felt a murderous rage take hold of him.

Dottie pulled back from the window when she saw Angel looking up at her. She put out the cigarette in the metal ashtray and walked back into the living room. Why was she so frightened? She heard the downstairs front door open and close. She could hear Angel's footsteps on the staircase. His parents' apartment was right across the hall from hers.

Angel was almost at the top of the stairs. Dottie's front door was right at the top of the stairs. The young man's footsteps stopped in front of her door.

Angel stood in front of Dottie's door for several minutes. Dottie Mendez was on the point of screaming. She put her hand to her mouth. Why should she scream? The young man was just standing there. Why was he standing there? He had caught her spying on him and wanted to teach her a lesson. Of course. That must be it. Should she open the door and confront him? No. A locked door stood between the two of them and she wanted to keep it that way.

-For God's sake, enough is enough. Christ!

She heard him move away from her door and enter his own apartment.

Dottie must have dozed off for at least a couple of hours, but she couldn't remember having actually slept. It didn't matter. She could now get dressed and get herself off to work. She worked at an insurance company in mid-town Manhattan in the Cash Settlement Dept. She hated the job, her manager, and most of her co-workers. Her life had been made miserable by the job's inflexible hours and low pay. She could barely meet her expenses much less save any decent amount of money. But, the hour long subway ride was better than staying alone in her empty and cold apartment. Maybe…just maybe, she ought to think about moving back home with her sisters and mother.

At about half past seven, she was locking her apartment door and getting ready to go out. The door to the apartment across the hall opened and out walked her young neighbor, Mr. Angel Correa. Dottie held her breath while fumbling with her keys.

-You're gonna' lose those keys. Better put them in your pocketbook.

Dottie did just that.

-Thanks. You're up early, handsome.

-Not really. I start at the gym before nine to avoid the morning rush.

-I didn't know that.

-Why should you? We've never spoken.

-How's mom and dad? I haven't seen them, lately.

-My dad's a cripple. You know that. And, my mom looks after him. I do most of the shopping for her. How come you're asking?

For the life of her, Dottie couldn't think of an answer. She nodded and started walking down the stairs. Angel followed her.

-You going into the city? I didn't think people were still working.

-This gal is. It may be the end of the world, but the landlord still wants the rent.

Dottie's self effacing humor was returning to her.

-I know what you mean. I still have to work out to be competitive. So, you think it's the end of the world? Am I wasting my time?

-Looks like it. But, they say the sun just might do a re-appearing act.

-I'd like to know why it disappeared in the first place.

-Wouldn't we all? Do you take my train, the M, into the city?

-No. I leave you at the corner and walk up to the LL subway. It takes me right outside my gym on 8th Ave. I don't mind the long ride. And, the trains have been kind of empty, lately, so I get to sit down and read the paper. I think maybe people are preparing for the end. They want to be with their families. I can respect that.

They reached the corner.

-You want to ask me something?

-Dottie's the name. Mind if I call you Angel?

-That's my name; but, I'm no angel if you get my drift.

-You saw me looking out my window last night. Couldn't sleep.

-I had trouble sleeping, too. I hung out on the stoop until I was good and tired. It's real easy to lose track of the time these last couple of days.

-I saw a man talking with you, Angel. Was he a friend of yours? Is he from around here? There was something creepy about him.

-Never saw him before. He was an ugly bastard. I really shouldn't say that, it's not nice. He must have had some kind of real bad accident. He was trying to warn me about something, but I'm not sure what. I had trouble understanding him.

Dottie had to ask her next question. They couldn't just stand at the corner much longer looking at each other.

-Angel, why were you standing in front of my door last night?

He looked her straight in the eye

-I was deciding whether or not to kill you.

PART IV

THE BLACK DISC
December 15 & 16, 1947

CHAPTER THIRTEEN

EDWARD TURNED over in bed to face Yolanda. He put his arms around her warm, naked body. So good. He drove his rod into that moist pussy and she, of course, responded.

-When you come don't take it out. Please! Never take it out!

Slowly and rhythmically and hard...his rod wanted to never stop pounding into her. Now, he was on top of her and he couldn't hold back. Some things are just impossible.

-Here it comes, baby!

He reached climax and lay on top of her for a while.

-Keep it in. You promised.

-I've gotta' pull out.

Edward pulled his rod out and let out a deep and satisfied groan.

-I needed that. Thanks, baby.

Yolanda smiled at him.

-So did I. Edward? Your body smells so nice with the new after shave I bought you.

He kissed her.

-Wouldn't leave home without it.

The P. I. got up to get a fresh pack of cigarettes. He found what he was after. Naked, he walked back to bed. He was loosing his erection.

-Want one?

Yolanda sighed contentedly and reached for his rod.

-Cigarette?

-What else?

-No, thanks. But, get back into bed, please. We have to talk.

Edward plopped back into bed, lit up and rubbed himself against his girlfriend.

-That feels nice, Edward.

-So, talk.

They were in Marlena's house in one of the spare bedrooms. Yolanda looked over at the alarm clock set on the small end table: 7:00 A.M. She reached over for her lipstick and compact: Coty. It was the only brand she used and she had tried most brands of cosmetics.

-We have to get the spear, Edward. I don't have to tell you that; and it better be today.

-That could be mighty dangerous. But, you're right. It's a chance we'll have to take.

The P. I. took a deep breath.

-And when we get it — *if* we get it — what the hell do we do with the damned thing. Any ideas?

-I don't know. Maybe just point it skyward toward the sun.

Edward smiled and stroked her wet spot.

-That's not a bad idea. Makes sense. Who *does* know for sure?

-That man, Holderman, from the book shop. He probably knows.

-That thug won't tell us anything. Forget it.

-Marlena?

-She knew about it, baby. She admitted that much last night. But, as usual, she's holding back.

-She said that only initiates could use it safely.

-Is she an initiate?

-I doubt it and not that she wouldn't want to be. Give me a drag on your cigarette, please?

He handed her his cigarette.

-There might be a way to gain some first hand knowledge about the spear.

-Oh? From whom? A Lodge member? Didn't your mother mention a Mr. Montenegro?

-I could track down the guy, but it might take too long. No. The person I had in mind is my dearly departed father: Mr. Manuel Mendez. How about a seance to get in touch with the old boy? I'm not crazy about the idea, but it's a thought.

-A seance can be dangerous. Have you ever been to one?

-I want to say no, but-

-Where would we hold it?

-At my mother's house this evening.

-Why not at the mausoleum where your father is interred? If his spirit is anywhere, it's there.

-Too close to a spear that could be deadly. Are you game?

-Of course. I've been to seances. And, you mentioned that you'd been to one, too. Besides, we haven't much time left. It has to be today.

-You're not kidding. According to Lt. Donovan, we've got about five days left if we're lucky.

The radiator in the room started clanking.

-The heat's coming up.

-It's late December, baby, so it should be coming up.

-We'd better get dressed and have something to eat. Do you think Marlena will want to come to the seance tonight?

-Probably. We'll ask her and Susan just to be polite. After breakfast, I want to head over to the 86th St. precinct and check in with Donovan. We could use his help and I want to know the results of that autopsy on Hoffman. It might tell us something.

Yolanda got out of bed.

-I don't like that Lt. Donovan.

-I know you don't. You stay here with Marlena and Susan. I'll pick you up when I come back and we'll head over to my mother's place. Donovan can drive me to where I parked my car.

Edward walked into the 86th precinct: it was only a few blocks from Marlena's townhouse; but Yolanda had insisted on calling him a cab just to play it safe. The precinct was a four story building with a red brick-face that has just been repointed.

The P. I. walked up to the front desk and asked for Lt. Donovan. The desk sergeant pointed toward the staircase just to the right behind a set of desks. There were police officers behind each desk interviewing people and writing notes of what was being said. The people being interviewed looked more like worried, everyday citizens than suspects or criminals. The entire floor was a scene of ordered chaos with officers and civilian workers moving about giving or following orders. All the overhead lights were burning.

Edward climbed the stairs. When he reached the second floor, he caught sight of Lt. Donovan's office. The commotion on this floor matched that of downstairs: shouting between cops and paperwork being written up and filed, and this time Edward saw suspects in handcuffs getting grilled. He threaded his way through the maze of desks and chairs.

He knocked on the frosted glass door.

-Come in.

Edward walked in, took off his hat and unbuttoned his overcoat.

-Hello, Mendez. Take a load off your feet.

Edward sat down in a straight back, wooden chair. Lt. Donovan's office was a lot tidier than he had expected. The desk had piles of neatly stacked papers on a green ink blotter along with a green baize lamp and inkwell. His typewriter was to the left of his desk on a small, portable tray. The office was small, but the window behind the desk was big: the bottom part having been flung open. The radiator pipes were right underneath the window and the steam was rising to the ceiling.

-Detective, I think it's time we compared notes.

-We did that last night, shamus. Anything happen since then that I oughta' know about? Cigarette?

-Thanks. My old brand: Lucky Strike.

He lit up and took a drag.

-I'll make this brief. My car was almost run off the road last night on my way downtown. Yolanda and I had to abandon it and take to the subway.

Lt. Donovan took this bit of information in.

-Were you followed down there?

-I'll say! They looked like a man and woman: professional assassins, both of them. We managed to dodge the bastards, but it was touch and go.

-Any connection to Hoffman's murder?

-I'd say yes.

Edward filled Lt. Donovan in on the details.

-Cold and ice: that's the connection. It's what ties all this damned business together. The temperature around the world is starting to drop, Mendez. Did you know that? It'll drop below freezing tonight. That just came in over the wireless a few minutes ago.

Edward nodded.

-Time's running out real fast.

-So, Mendez, what's our next move before we all freeze to death? I take that back. I know what it is.

-Clue me in, Lieutenant, 'cause I don't.

-I've got a lead on Hoffman's murder. A suspect was seen leaving his apartment just about the time of the killing. We tracked him down. Want to tag along and meet him?

-You bet. Any word on that autopsy?

-Hoffman was frozen to death and suffocated. It wasn't instantaneous, either. That would account for the look on the poor bastard's face.

-But, what generated so much cold? How was it done?

-Forensics is still working on that. Maybe if we could catch your two subway pursuers, they could tell us.

He got up and put on his suit jacket.

-Let's head on over to the interrogation room. I'll do all the talking.

The two men left the small office and made their way up to the third floor. There was less chaos up there and a few more private rooms.

-In there. He's an arrogant prick.

The two men entered the interrogation room: a room with a square wooden table and one overhead light. There were several wooden chairs set around the table. A police officer was standing next to a seated man in handcuffs. The handcuffed man and the police officer turned to look at the two men who had just entered. The officer nodded to Lt. Donovan. The suspect started at seeing Edward.

-You! I know you.

-You sure do, pal.

The suspect was Wulf Holderman from the book shop. He didn't look too happy about his present situation.

Lt. Donovan looked hard at Edward.

-You two gentlemen know each other?

-We met yesterday morning. Mr. Holderman, here, needed to be taught a lesson on how to treat a lady.

-You pulled a gun on me.

-You remember.

Lt. Donovan interrupted.

-That's enough, boys.

The Lieutenant sat down opposite Holderman. Edward placed a chair in the far corner and put his hat on, brim down, so that the suspect couldn't make out his face in the dimly lit room.

Lt. Donovan started the interrogation.

-You're name's Wulf Holderman?

-You know this.

-Don't let me ask it a second time.

-Yes.

-Are you a citizen of the United States?

-I seek to emigrate to your country.

-So, you're not a citizen. Any relatives in New York City?

-None.

-Friends?

-None.

-Must be lonely for you. When did you arrive in the city?

-I first came to New York in 1923 and remained for a short time under a visitor's visa. I returned here last year.

-Take your time, pal. Why were you here in 1923?

-Simply to visit your country and to check out any possible business opportunities that I might take advantage of.

-Did you know Werner Hoffman at that time?

-Our paths had crossed; but, we were never friends.

-What's your present occupation?

-I own a book shop on 18th St. here in the city

-Any employees?

-No.

-How's business?

-It comes and goes. Lately, it is non-existent.

-What are you doing for money?

-I have some saved.

-We'll get back to that last statement.

Lt. Donovan made a point of studying the tip of his cigarette.

-When had young Hoffman been to your book shop?

-The previous evening. It was shortly after the sun's light had been extinguished.

Lt. Donovan cracked a smile.

-Oh? Like I'm about to extinguish this cigarette?

And, with that, he reached across the table and put out the lighted cigarette on Holderman's hand. The suspect cursed his interrogator and rubbed the injured hand.

-You capitalist bastard! Is this the typical American police tactics? They stink.

-I couldn't find an ashtray. I didn't want to use *my* hand.

-Pig!

Edward had leaned forward in his chair, but said nothing.

-You had a lot of money on you, pal: five grand to be exact. You usually carry that much change around?

-That's none of your business.

-I'm making it my business. Where'd you get that kind of money? I don't hear you. That dump you call a book shop can't pay off that kind of dough.

-Go fuck yourself.

-Your hand still hurt?

-Go to hell.

-We're all headed for the deep freeze. I want to know where you got that kind of money from. *Where?* Don't let me ask again.

-I earned it.

-Doing what? What the fuck did you do to earn that kind of bread?

-I baked it.

-Your hand still hurt?

-I'm used to pain.

-What were you doing at Werner Hoffman's apartment last night?

-I had business with the young man.

-What sort of business?

-He was looking for a particular book on the lost continent of Atlantis. I couldn't locate it for him; but, I did recommend a few other titles. There are many.

-Why not just phone him?

-I knew his father back in Germany. So, I decided to pay the son a call. I was lonely. I didn't stay long. I don't indulge in small talk.

-When did you get there and when did you leave? That's two questions.

-I can count. It was about seven o'clock when I arrived. It's hard to tell time with this current phenomenon. I never carry a watch on me, anyway. I stayed maybe ten minutes, but no longer. He was alive when I left.

Edward took note of that last answer: it had to be a lie.

-Do you live at your book shop?

-In the back. As I said, money is tight. I had to withdraw all of my savings; that's how I came to have so much money on me.

Edward smirked at that. It took him long enough to think of a half plausible lie. Lt. Donovan must have had the same thought.

The police lieutenant placed a gun on to the table.

-Belong to you?

-You know that it does.

-Got a license for it?

-Not in this country.

-You don't have a license for it. We're gonna' have to hold you, Mr. Holderman, for illegal possession.

Edward got up and walked over to the Lieutenant.

-See me outside for a second?

-Excuse me, Mr. Holderman?

The suspect didn't answer.

Out in the hallway:

-What is it, Mendez?

-I've got a favor to ask.

-Ask it.

-I want to pay a visit to that book shop.

-I'll lend you Holderman's keys. We might tell him about it later or never. Surprised I said yes?

-I'm glad you said yes. Thanks.

-The world's almost out of time. We gotta' stretch the rules to the max. And, that bastard in there knows a lot more than he's telling. As soon as I'm done with him, I'll get you the keys. Sergeant Rayno can drive you to your car on Columbus. Let me know what you find.

-I will. I'll give the place a good going over. And, thanks, again.

In half an hour, Edward was getting back in his own car that he'd hastily parked on Columbus Circle last night. Sergeant Tom Rayno had driven him down in a squad car and the two men had gotten acquainted. They had a mutual passion for ice hockey and American history. Only one problem: Sergeant Rayno was a nonsmoker. Edward didn't hold this against the young man.

As the P. I. pulled out of his parking space on Columbus, he noticed that Sergeant Rayno was tailing him.

-I guess Donovan wants two versions. Fair enough.

It didn't take long for him to reach 18th and 5th. He pulled up in front of the book shop and his friendly "tail" parked on the opposite side of the street.

Edward got out of his Ford and locked up. He fumbled with the keys to the front door of the book shop. He found the right one and the lock clicked open. Sergeant Rayno got out of the squad car and gestured for Edward to go into the book shop. The P. I. smiled and waved back.

-A bodyguard. Well, what do you know about that? And, he likes ice hockey.

Edward entered the shop and closed the door behind him. His eyes adjusted to the darkness as he made his way to the back. He glanced at the books along the walls: all of them looked so old and, yet, well kept. He ran his finger over one shelf and found not a speck of dust on it. Holderman was tidy.

-And, to think, I thought he was a slob.

The P. I. reached the door to the back room. He placed one hand on the doorknob and the other on his gun. He pushed open the door and fumbled for the light switch on the wall, but couldn't find it. He could just make out an overhead light with a cord dangling from it, so he pulled on it. The light came on: it was harsh and yellow and for just a second, Edward was blinded by its light.

A man was sitting in the corner. It looked like-

-Werner Hoffman? It can't be. You come back from the dead or something?

-I *am* Werner Hoffman. Please, lower your gun. I pose no danger.

-Forget it, pal.

The P. I. leaned closer to the man sitting down.

-Hold on. Who are you? Give.

This man looked considerably older than Edward's client of three days ago. The face was lined and the blonde hair was grey at the temples and thinning.

-I told you. I am Werner Hoffman, Sr.

-His father! But, he said you were dead. Was your son in the habit of lying?

-I'm as good as dead. We all are. The filth who were once my comrades is after me...the filth beneath the earth. It is they who killed my son. It is they, Mr. Mendez, who will kill us all.

-Your son told you about me?

-It was I who sent him to you. I'm acquainted with your sister, Nella Mendez. I knew your father, Manuel Mendez.

-Tell me about that.

-We belonged to the same brotherhood that has no name. It is a brotherhood which no longer exists.

-You sure about that because I'm not.

-Its members are scattered throughout various countries. By themselves, they wield little power. I know this.

-Thirty years ago, you placed your son in foster care. Why, Mr. Hoffman? What made you do that?

-For his own protection. I had not the means to look after him properly. Our leader, who was your father, was dying. We knew why.

-The spear.

-Yes. The spear that infected his blood. The spear that must now be found.

-Where is it?

-Lost.

-You must have some idea.

-Do *you*, Mr. Mendez? I think that you do.

-Maybe.

-You mustn't touch it. Heed that warning.

-Why not?

-It killed your father. It has killed others.

-You just said that we had to find it.

-We must.

Mr. Hoffman, Sr. was trembling.

-But, if we can't handle it-

-I will be the one to use it. My life is all but over.

-Will the spear bring back the sun? Is it that powerful?

-The sun has been shifted to another dimension: a parallel universe. However, the transference is not stable. In time, it will return to its original and fixed position.

-Then, why bother with the spear? Let's just leave it where it is.

-No. It must be found and quickly. The sun *will* re-appear eventually, but for mankind it will be too late. They will then take over the earth.

-They?

-The Nazis who made it to Antarctica. It is they who shifted the sun, but the transference is unstable, too much energy is needed to maintain it.

-Are these Nazis amongst us now, Mr. Hoffman?

-Yes. They are ruthless murderers who have gained the secrets of a lost and unknown civilization: the ancestors of the Sumerians.

Edward leaned against the far wall. He tried to absorb everything that he'd just heard. The front door opened and a voice called out.

-Mendez? You okay?

The P. I. shouted back.

-I'm back here. Just walk straight back, Sergeant.

Sergeant Rayno walked to where Edward and Hoffman were.

-Who's this?

-Mr. Werner Hoffman, Sr.

-Hoffman's old man?

-The same. I think you might want to take him in for some questioning, Sergeant.

-Mr. Hoffman? Come with me, please?

Werner Hoffman, Sr. stood up and faced Edward.

-But, Mr. Mendez, I thought we had an agreement.

-It's for your own protection. Don't argue.

-You need my help.

-I might. But, for now, I need you safe. You go ahead with Sergeant Rayno. He'll take you to his precinct and look after you. Sergeant? Hand Mr. Hoffman over to Lt. Donovan.

-You bet. Mr. Hoffman, we'll need you for questioning and identification.

-I'll lock up here, Sergeant.

The three men walked to the front of the book shop with Mr. Hoffman in front of Sgt. Rayno and Edward bringing up the rear.

Outside on the sidewalk, the P. I. locked the front door and walked over to his car. Sgt. Rayno had driven off with Mr. Hoffman. Edward took out a cigarette and lit up. He intended to head back to Marlena's and pick up Yolanda. He took a drag on his cigarette and exhaled. Better. There was a movement close to him and the scent of perfume.

-Okay. Let me see you. Quit playing hide-and-seek.

A woman emerged from the darkness. She was petite and had short, dark hair. She carried a small purse in her hand and a cigarette in the other.

-You got a name, lady?

-But, of course. Perhaps, you know of me. I am Nathalie Montaigne. I know Werner Hoffman.

It took Edward a couple of seconds to recognize the name of this heavily made-up woman.

-My former client mentioned you. You're the Frenchwoman his father knew in Germany.

-You say "former client." Is young Werner no longer your client?

-He's dead.

She made the sign of the cross.

-Mon Dieu! It is just as I feared. I was on my way into the book shop when I saw the three of you emerge. I was at a loss as to what to do.

-You've got your own key?

-Yes. All members are welcome.

-I thought women were personae-non-gratis.

-Not this woman. Always, there are exceptions to rules.

-How do you know me?

-You resemble your father. He was known to me. And, now, you must take me with you for it is unsafe in the dark streets. I don't know what the father has told you, Mr. Mendez, but I have much to say to you. Both our lives are in terrible danger. Please, let us get into your automobile. It's dangerous to be exposed like this.

Edward opened the door on the passenger side of the car. Nathalie climbed in and locked the door. The P. I. walked around to the driver's side and did likewise. He started up the engine and pulled out.

-A cigarette, cherie? My last one is almost extinguished.

He offered the lady a cigarette. She accepted the Lucky Strike and lit up.

-Nice tobacco. I like American cigarettes. The taste is not as harsh as European cigarettes and the paper is superior.

-Nathalie, where are you staying?

-I was staying with young Hoffman. I dare not go back there now or they'd kill me for sure. How was he killed? Frozen to death, no doubt? It's their usual method.

-You know as much as I do.

-Ghastly! A horrible way to die. The pigs were looking for the spear, surely. But, I happen to know that young Werner didn't have it.

-He didn't.

-And, now we must find the artifact, no?

-I'd say, yes. And, we don't have too much time for small talk or past events.

-Go on, cherie.

-We need to get that spear and…I just might know where it is.

Nathalie turned to look at the P. I., who in turn was gauging her reaction to his loaded statement.

-You are most well informed. Where is it?

Edward evaded the question.

-I'm going to pick up my girlfriend and from there, we'll be going to my mother's place in Brooklyn. I plan on holding a seance. We need help. Wanna' come?

-To contact your dead father, no doubt.

Now, she stared straight ahead.

-You know that to handle the spear is dangerous: quite deadly, in fact, even for initiates.

-That's the reason for the seance. I've got a gut feeling that my old man handled that spear…and knew just how to do it. He did live to a ripe old age.

Nathalie reached into her bag and took out some gum.

-A piece, cherie?

-Thanks.

-I will come. I met your mother once a long time ago. Did you know that?

-There's an awful lot I don't know.

-Count yourself lucky.

Edward turned the car on to Times Square and headed west.

-Would you turn up the heat, please? It's quite cold.

-You're right. I'll turn on the heater. Temperature must be dropping outside.

-How frightening to have no sun in the sky. Have you heard that the planet might actually move out of its orbit? We'll all be dead, for sure, if that catastrophe should happen.

Edward didn't answer. Instead, he turned on the car's heater and switched on the radio.

"The Mayor and his advisors are now in session. All day, there's been a rumor of Marshall Law being put into effect. The official announcement should come soon.

"Temperatures are dropping around the globe. Snow has begun to fall in northern Europe and along the Mongolian regions. Canada has also reported blizzard-like conditions in northern Quebec and Edmonton."

Edward turned off the radio. They were just past 57th St.

-We'll be there in a few minutes. Nathalie? Do we need to know anything else? Do you know what to do with the spear because I sure don't.

-I've never actually seen it, but I know who last possessed it.

-Who?

The Frenchwoman hesitated a second before answering.

-Your father, of course.

-You were gonna' say something else.

-No. I wasn't.

Edward didn't believe her.

-Lady, what kind of a chump do you take me for?

CHAPTER FOURTEEN

EDWARD AND his French passenger arrived at Marlena's townhouse to be greeted by a nervous Yolanda. She'd been pacing the floor of the dark corridor leading to the front door. Where was her boyfriend and why was he taking so long? She didn't like being by herself in Marlena's place. There was no telling who might try to get in.

-Edward, I don't know where Marlena and Susan went. I don't think that Susan even knew. Her mother was in a big hurry and said that there was no time to wait for you. They wanted me to go with them; but, I didn't think that would be fair to you. I have the spare key to lock up.

-She probably took her gun with her, as well.

Edward made the appropriate introductions. Nathalie needed to go to the powder room. Yolanda showed her the way and then came back down to Edward.

-Who is she? Can we trust her?

-She's a member of my father's Lodge or so she claims. And, no, I don't trust her. That's why I'm keeping a close eye on her. She appeared a little too conveniently out of nowhere.

Edward looked around the dark living room. He didn't like this house. It had too many secrets and it was always so damned, friggin' dark!

-We're gonna head to my mother's place, baby, and have ourselves that seance.

Yolanda looked into Edward's dark brown eyes.

-I don't like that. You never know what's going to happen or to whom. Do we really need to do this?

-My old man's gotta' help us.

-To do what? We know where the spear is. We don't need his help for that. And, why should we bring this stranger with us?

-It's lethal to handle, and I don't want to die if I don't have to. After the seance, we'll go-

Edward looked up. Nathalie had walked back into the living room. How much of their conversation had she overheard? He looked past Yolanda.

-Nathalie, you all set to go?

-I am, cherie. I'm glad you parked your vehicle just outside. Those killers are probably nearby.

-Okay, ladies, time to lock up and head on over to Brooklyn.

Yolanda tucked her arm into Edward's.

-I hope we're doing the right thing. I'm still not sure that we have to.

-Neither am I, baby. Let's not waste any more time, though. We've gotta' do *something*.

Marlena and Susan were headed to Staten Island. Susan was driving their Bentley because her mother was too reckless with the car. Marlena had been involved in several minor accidents over the last couple of years and her driver's license had almost been suspended. They and their car were now being moved across the bay by the Staten Island ferry. Marlena was eating a Fifth Avenue candy bar and offered her daughter a piece which she accepted.

-Thanks. I think we're about halfway across the bay. We should be at the terminal in ten minutes or so.

-Not soon enough. It's getting colder: a most dreadful and penetrating chill.

The two of them buttoned up their insulated trench coats to the top button. Susan adjusted her silk scarf while her mother put on her leather gloves The overhead light in the car was turned on, but it was still dark: each passenger was a dark silhouette to the other.

-We should have waited for Edward, mother. He might have had some important information for us.

-We'll see him later back at the house. This trip couldn't wait; and there was no telling when the dear boy would be back. I'd just heard over the news that a blizzard is about to hit the city.

-I didn't hear that this morning.

-It wasn't on the radio this morning. The earth is losing its internal heat and the weather is changing more rapidly than can be reported.

Susan was tempted to turn on the radio, but she resisted the impulse.

-Mother? Dare I ask why we're headed to this occult Lodge? What do you hope to find there and please give me a direct answer.

-Information, of course.

-Specifics, please?

-Getting the spear is only the first step. It's a weapon and a dangerous one. We must know what to do with it and what not to do with it. It must be used but when and where? Is there a specific point on the planet where it must be placed? To get the spear and not know would be like dropping an atomic bomb at random.

Susan laughed.

-I did ask, didn't I?

Susan sat back and stared ahead at the parked car in front of them, but her thoughts were of her mother sitting next to her. Everything she did was centered around her mother; all her research work and studies were influenced or directed by her mother. The papers she had published in occult and scientific journals had all been initiated under the aegis of Marlena Lake. The daughter was not complaining. Her life was interesting and well directed and, thanks to her late father's inheritance, she had money of her own.

Tonight, Susan had on her usual pants and tweed jacket with her trench coat for added warmth. She favored mens' garments and rarely wore a dress. Her make-up was minimal; but, she did allow herself the indulgence of expensive French perfume. At the moment, she was trying out a new fragrance: Miss Dior. She smiled at her own perceived weakness.

-Did you feel that, mother? The boat is docking.

The ferry boat maneuvered into the docking area between the two wood pilings.

Before leaving Marlena's, Edward had called his sister, Nella, and told her that they were on their way. He didn't mention the seance or Nathalie. His car was now pulling up in front of the red brick row house. He and Yolanda were up front with Nathalie in the back seat.

-I hate to leave this warm and comfortable car, Mr. Mendez. You drive quite skillfully.

-It'll be warm inside. Let's go on in, ladies.

The three people made their way up the stoop. Edward knocked on the door and Nella opened it.

-Please, come in.

They entered the small foyer. Nella took the ladies' coats. Edward hung up his own overcoat and hat. They went into the living room where Edward stopped dead in his tracks.

-Mother! What in the world are you doing out of your bedroom? No wonder the world's coming to an end.

Mrs. Mendez was sitting in an easy chair near the fireplace. She was wearing a black, cotton dress with white lace trimmings. She smiled at her son.

-Good evening, Edward. Yes. I've emerged from my sanctuary. Had I reason to? Tell me. But, first introduce me to your two lady friends.

The P. I. made the introductions.

-Have we met before, Miss Montaigne?

-Yes, Mrs. Mendez. It was many years ago at a gathering in this very house. I'm flattered that you remember the occasion.

-We must speak later on. You knew the Hoffmans?

-Yes. I knew the father quite well, if you get my drift.

-I do.

Victoria came in carrying a tea service. She put it down on the coffee table and began pouring tea for everyone. Nella helped her to serve.

With the exception of Edward, everyone was seated and sipping tea when they heard footsteps coming down the stairs. It was Edward's eldest sister, Catrina. Edward went to greet her even though he didn't like her. She was tall and too thin in his own opinion. The make-up she wore gave her a hard appearance and her hair was lacquered into place. Her demeanor and character matched this masque.

Edward took a good, hard look at his sister and thought of a passage from the Bible: the fatted calf. She was the proverbial fatted calf to be led to the slaughter. The pampering, the parental indulgences...eat, drink and be merry for tomorrow, dear sister, you'll be dead or worse. His mother knew it…and Catrina knew it. Always fleeing from place to place and always coming back to her destiny. What that was, Edward didn't know. He didn't want to know.

The P. I. extended his hand to his sister.

-Catrina, haven't seen you for quite a while. Didn't know your were back in town.

In her usual clipped tongue, the eldest sister answered her brother.

-I've come to visit mother. I'll be leaving tomorrow afternoon if I can get a flight out.

Yolanda had been watching this little scene. With a smile, she told Catrina the bad news.

-Haven't you heard? All flights have been cancelled.

Catrina glared at the figure skater and brushed past Edward.

-I don't believe you. Who are you?

Not waiting for an answer, she turned on her brother.

-Who have you brought here to my mother's house? Strangers?

Edward introduced Yolanda and Nathalie.

Catrina continued her tirade.

-All flights have been cancelled? Why? When did this happen?

Yolanda looked her straight in the face.

-A few hours ago. There was a terrible mid-air collision over Chicago. At least one hundred people were killed. And, there've been reports of other flights missing.

Mrs. Mendez spoke to no one in particular.

-Horrible. Something must be done. But, is it already too late?

Yolanda spoke to Mrs. Mendez. She was starting to like Edward's mother.

-I don't think it is, Mrs. Mendez, and neither does Edward. We have to try. We can't just wait around for the end of the world.

-You're right, of course. I wouldn't have left my room otherwise. I like your spirit, young lady. You must be quite the competitor on the ice.

Catrina interrupted.

-Mother, should you be up? I'll help you back to your room.

-No. Catrina. I'm not the least bit tired.

Victoria picked up her teacup.

-Eddie, we finally got a hold of Dottie. She's okay and just plain scared like the rest of us.

-I'll try and drop by her place, if I can.

Nathalie, who was just finishing her tea, spoke up.

-Mr. Mendez, perhaps we should tell your mother and sisters why we are here tonight? We've really no time for pleasantries.

Edward was annoyed. He'd planned on making the announcement in his own time.

-Yes, Edward, why are you here?

That was Catrina speaking. She had placed herself behind her mother's armchair.

-To save the world, lady, or at least to take a stab at it.

Edward took out a cigarette and lit up. Yolanda got up and stood next to her boyfriend. She put her hand on his shoulder and whispered.

-Don't let that bitch provoke you. Your mother is on our side.

Mrs. Mendez addressed her son.

-How can we save ourselves, Edward? And, why do I feel as if I already know?

-With your permission, we'll need to hold a seance, mother.

Victoria dropped her empty cup on to the rug.

-Oh, that sounds too frightening.

Catrina addressed her brother.

-I won't permit it. How dare you even suggest such an unholy thing? Must I order you out of this house? It's obscene.

Mrs. Mendez put an end to her oldest daughter's protest.

-Catrina, this is *my* house and you will show more respect to your brother and his guests.

-But, mother-

-Please, Catrina. Don't you realize that something must be done to reverse what has happened? Science alone cannot do it, but there are other means, aren't there, Edward?

-I hope so.

-You are your father's son and a gifted occultist even if you do not yet realize it.

-I'm a P. I., mother. I love my work.

-Indeed. Miss Montaigne, you want to say something?

-Nathalie. I am a foreigner in your country, but I will speak freely. The seance must be held tonight for there would have been a full moon in the night sky; that full moon can still afford us some measure of its protection.

Catrina addressed her brother in a sneering tone of voice.

-Whom are we to contact? Will any spirit do, dear brother? One assumes that you know.

Edward tried holding on to his patience with his eldest sister. What he wanted to do was give her a good kick up the backside and dislodge that bug up her ass. Yolanda squeezed his hand.

-Catrina, no one here will force you to participate. We're going through with it so get used to the idea and *shut up!* We've got mother's permission. We don't need yours.

That closing statement brought a smile to Edward's face. He sent out a puff of smoke in Catrina's direction.

Victoria, who had scooped up her tea cup, leaned forward in her chair.

-Eddie? I'm kind of scared, but I still want to join in. I'm too afraid not to. Who are we going to contact? Can you tell us?

Edward looked at his pretty sister.

-Our late father, Victoria: Mr. Manuel Mendez.

CHAPTER FIFTEEN

SUSAN PULLED out of the ferry terminal and drove on to Bay Street. At first, the driving wasn't difficult. There were street lamps on every corner and the office buildings near the terminal had most of their lights turned on: artificial light to keep out the darkness. The headlights of the car were beams of penetrating light that at least illuminated the roadway ahead.

The two women drove down Bay Street toward Highland Blvd; there were no more office buildings and only the occasional residence. The driving became more difficult; between the beacons of the lamp posts were stretches of pitch blackness.

Marlena looked out in disapproval on the landscape.

-How can anyone live in this godforsaken place?

-It's probably the isolation that's the appealing factor. I wish Edward were with us. He knows this area infinitely better than we do.

-Look! It's starting to snow.

Susan rolled her eyes.

-That's all we need.

-It's a light snowfall. Interesting how the night sky is so brilliant and such a contrast to the blackness surrounding us.

-I'll say! Look for the turn off, mother. It should be close to Edward's apartment, I think.

-I still have the key to that apartment. If we have to, we can stay there for the night.

-I'd rather not. I wouldn't feel safe there so cut-off from civilization.

-Then, step on that gas pedal, young lady. There's been no traffic in either direction on this roadway. It should be safe enough.

Susan stepped on the gas pedal and also turned on the windshield wipers.

-What brazen arrogance. To think that you can save the world when scientists around the globe are baffled. You disgust me. I won't permit this blasphemous outrage.

Yolanda had just about enough of this bitch.

-Oh? And, do you have any better ideas? You don't. At least, we're willing to try and take a risk. We know the danger.

Catrina glared at the beautiful figure skater with undisguised jealousy.

-How dare you?

Mrs. Mendez stepped in.

-Enough of this. This is my house and we will go through with the seance. Edward, it's how one must handle the spear; that is the purpose of all this.

-Yes, mother. There must be a way. Father was able to handle it, at least for a short time, anyway.

Nathalie spoke to the matriarch.

-Mrs. Mendez, Yolanda is right; a seance can be dangerous. We must warn you of this danger. We seek your husband, but others may answer the call.

-I've already made up my mind. We'll conduct the seance in the dining room. The table is made of oak and it is round. We have enough chairs.

Catrina was close to hysterics.

-Mother, I won't allow this.

-Catrina, you have no say in the matter. Go to your room, if you wish. No one is forcing you to participate. And, in your present state of mind, you should *not* participate.

The eldest sister turned her back on everyone and hurried up the stairs. Her bedroom door slammed shut.

Victoria laughed.

-Let's just hope she stays locked up.

Edward spoke to Nella who had been quiet throughout most of the conversation.

-Nella, you'd better go up and tell her to stay in her room. It'd be just like her to come down later and louse things up.

-I will. And, we're better off without her. She's probably more frightened than anyone. It's a shame that she can't admit to her fear.

Nella went upstairs. They could her hear knocking on Catrina's bedroom door. It was opened and voices could be heard.

-My big sister can handle Catrina. Why don't we all move into the dining room? Mother, let me help you. Sorry about the cigarette smoke.

-I don't mind. Your father was a heavy smoker.

Edward and his mother led the way into the adjoining dining room: a small room with no windows. However, one could see through to the outside world via the living room windows.

Edward helped his mother into a chair. Yolanda sat to Mrs. Mendez's left and Edward left a chair for himself to his mother's right. Victoria sat next to Yolanda and Nathalie was next to the figure skater. Nella would be sitting between Edward and Nathalie.

The P. I. removed the lace tablecloth and placed a brass candle holder in the center of the oak table. He went back into the living room to wait for Nella to come downstairs. He could hear her and Catrina arguing.

Susan reached into the glove compartment for a flashlight. What she also found was an assortment of candy bars that her mother had stashed there: a box of Dots, Turkish Taffy, a box of Whoppers Malted Milk Balls, Junior Mints, a Three Musketeers bar, a Heath candy bar and, Susan's favorite: a SkyBar. She reached further back and found the flashlight. The car was parked only a few yards from a deserted old house. It was too dark to make out any details of the building. All that could be seen was its silhouette against the falling snow.

-Mother, did Professor Lange actually say that beings from another planet founded the Sumerian race?

-He said that one of their cites still existed…well, just as good.

-And, you believed him? You can't be serious?

-At the time, I did not argue with him.

-And, now?

-The old fool was withholding information. He'll regret that.

-Then, pardon me for asking, but what are we doing out here in the dead of night in the middle of nowhere?

-Listen to mother: it's like reading a newspaper, my dear, you must read between the lines to get at the crux of the story.

-And, the crux of *this* story?

-The dear Professor belonged to an occult Lodge which I believe was associated with the Nazi regime.

-You mean that some Nazi contingent is behind all this? But, the technology to carry it out simply doesn't exist — at least not yet.

-The Nazis sent several expeditions down to Antarctica. Those south pole expeditions must have uncovered some lost technology of the ancients. I'm convinced of it.

-To commit global genocide?

-Yes. And, then, somehow reverse the process and reclaim the planet.

-Assuming that they're able to survive, how do they reverse it?

-By means of the Spear of Longinus; that must be it.

-We hope, but that's taking an awful risk. And, by the way, we have only the one flashlight.

-It will do. Let's go. We've wasted enough time.

The two women got out of the car and locked their respective doors. The snow was still coming down and the wind had picked up.

-This snow looks and feels more like tiny ice crystals.

-It is unusual and, perhaps, the first sign of the climatic change. Keep the flashlight's beam low to the ground, Susan. We don't want to announce our arrival.

Marlena turned around to make sure that they weren't being followed. She could see no one and there were no points of light to indicate any one approaching from the distance.

In another few minutes, they were climbing the wooden steps to the front door of the house.

-Perhaps, we should knock?

-Is my mother insane?

-Only joking. And, keep your voice down. I don't hear anyone walking about inside. I wonder if the door's open?

Marlena tried the door. Locked. She took out a thin, silver blade from her pocketbook. She inserted it into the lock of the door and it clicked open. She opened the door and beckoned her daughter to follow her inside.

CHAPTER SIXTEEN

NELLA CAME down the stairs and joined her brother in the living room.

-Edward, I told Catrina to stay in her room until you call for her. She wasn't too pleased about it; but when is she ever pleased?

-Too bad. But, will she do it?

-How long is the proverbial piece of string? It's a risk we'll have to take.

-Well, we can't worry about her now.

-What's wrong, Edward?

-I feel like I'm betraying my profession, Nella. I deal in facts and people, not seances and sacred objects.

-You *are* dealing in facts no matter how unorthodox it may seem. We must know for certain if the spear is lethal. And-

-Yes?

-It might not still be in the crypt with father. Have you thought of that? If the German Chancellor lost it,

why would it return to our father? *How* would it return to him?

Edward shrugged his broad shoulders.

-Beats me. But, you're right, Nella. You're always right. And, if it's not in the crypt, maybe our father can tell us where it is which is just one more reason to have this little seance of ours tonight.

He took his sister's hand.

-Come on. Let's go on in and join the others.

-Good boy.

Edward and Nella took their places at the dining room table. For a few moments, they sat in silence staring at the lighted candle that Mrs. Mendez had lit, each person gathering his and her strength.

-Edward, you will conduct the seance. You are your father's son. I feel that we must hurry.

Edward nodded in ascent to his mother and addressed the five women.

-Once we start, no one must utter a word. We'll touch fingertips and this circle mustn't be broken. If anything frightening or strange things happen just try to ignore it.

The seance began.

-We must send our thoughts into the realm which can't be seen. It's a realm...a universe that's parallel to this one...a different, phantasmic dimension that goes beyond the known four dimensions.

He took a deep breath.

-Father, hear your son calling to you. The world needs your help because without it we're doomed. Please, speak to me and tell us about the spear.

A silence descended upon the six people.

-Father, we need your help. Answer your son. I'm Edward.

The group of people stared at the candle. It glowed in a sea of darkness like a flame set adrift in the blackness of space.

Yolanda thought she heard something. It was someone coming down the stairs.

-It's that bitch, Catrina. She'll ruin everything.

She didn't give voice to her thoughts; but the noise had shifted her focus from where it should be. Nella glanced at the figure skater. She, too, had heard the footsteps on the staircase and knew who it was.

-My no good, interfering sister.

Like Yolanda, she kept her thoughts to herself.

Edward shifted in his chair as if in pain.

Nathalie wanted to speak, but knew enough to keep her mouth shut. Victoria was too frightened to say anything to anyone. Mrs. Mendez looked at Edward, wanting to help him and knowing that she couldn't.

Edward, who had closed his eyes now opened them.

-Look at the center of the table. Do you see it?

The five women turned to look. At first, they couldn't make out anything but utter blackness...a circle of blackness that was now spreading itself across the table.

Mrs. Mendez gasped.

-The candle- the flame is gone from the candle!

Nathalie leaned forward in her chair, horrified.

-The circle of death and blackness. I can see the very perimeter.

Yolanda stifled a scream as she turned to Edward.

-It's spreading out toward us. What can we do?

Edward shouted a warning.

-Don't move.

No one could. It was a force that chained them all together.

Nella spoke to no one in particular.

-It's some sort of unholy chasm.

Edward tried peering into the black hole.

-Something is moving in its depths. Whatever it is, it's alive.

-Edward, what do you see? I can't look.

-I can't make it out, Yolanda. It's just a ripple of movement. But, I've got my gun on me. If it's mortal, I'll be ready for it.

-Your gun will do you no good, cherie.

Nella spoke to her brother.

-Something is reaching out. It looks like an arm. It's coming closer. I can almost make out a face.

A black silhouette of an arm emerged from the center of the hole. It moved toward Edward.

This time Yolanda screamed.

-My God! It looks like Hitler. Edward! It's coming toward you. Get your gun out! Stop the seance.

It glided closer toward Edward. He tried to move but couldn't. His hands were bound to the table. He couldn't reach for his gun. The silhouette moved in an almost sensual manner as if it were "swimming" toward its prey.

Yolanda heard the door of the dining room open. Catrina stood in the doorway gazing at the black hole and the evil coming from out of its depths toward her brother. She screamed and ran toward the light switch, but her hand brushed against the edge of the black hole that had once been a dining room table. The black arm reached out and grabbed her by the wrist. Catrina was pulled into the black hole. She cried out for help as her body was dragged into and under the surface of infinity.

Edward stood up and looked into the chasm. He thought he saw Catrina's distorted and terrified face. He broke the circle and flipped on the light switch. The black hole vanished. The dining room table was there and so was the lighted candle. Catrina was gone.

Nella put both her hands to her face. Yolanda stared at the table, too afraid to even touch it. Victoria wanted to search the house for her vanished sister. Mrs. Mendez stared blindly at her pretty daughter knowing that any search would be useless.

Edward touched Yolanda's shoulder.

-I'm going to search the house. We have to. Stay in the living room with Nathalie. Nella? Help mother to her room. Victoria? You come with me.

Edward and Victoria went upstairs to search all the rooms and the attic. Nathalie spoke to Nella.

-I am a practical nurse. Let me help you with your mother. She's appears to be in shock. We need to get her to bed. And, if you can make some more of your delicious tea, cherie, that will help.

-Of course.

Nella and Nathalie helped Mrs. Mendez to her room. The elderly matriarch was beginning to recover from her ordeal. She whispered a few words to Nathalie.

-Catrina will not be in this house. Useless. Useless to search. My daughter is lost.

-I understand, Mrs. Mendez. And, most decidedly, you are correct, but one must go through the motions.

The three women exited the room.

Edward and Victoria reached the upstairs landing.

-Victoria, do you mind if I have a look around Catrina's room?

-You're asking me, Eddie? Why don't we both go in and explore the Princess' domain? See how the "other half" lives.

-You're on.

They walked into Catrina's bedroom. The lamp light by her bed was still on. Edward spoke first.

-This room is impeccably clean. It's like no one has ever set foot in it.

He turned to his sister.

-Victoria, has it always been like this?

-I really don't know. I never come in here. But, you're right Eddie...it's so cold and sterile. It gives me the creeps. Somehow, it doesn't go with the rest of the house, if that makes any sense.

Edward agreed. He opened the closet door.

-t's like some hotel room that no one's ever occupied. Take a look at the clothes, Victoria. Everything is in plastic garment bags.

He sat on the edge of the bed.

-Victoria? Where did Catrina travel to?

Victoria was going through the bureau drawers.

-I know that she's been to Europe several times. She'd send mother postcards and an occasional letter. She never sent the rest of us anything.

-Where to in Europe?

Victoria smiled.

-The three of us did read the postcards: it was mostly London. Catrina didn't speak any foreign languages…at least, not well enough to carry on a conversation.

-But, where did she go during the war? From what Nella tells me, she was never at home.

-She spent some time in Mexico City and San Francisco. Who knows what she did there? I don't.

-Mother would know. And, all those times in foreign places, but never any substantial amount of time in her own home. What the hell was she so terrified of?

Victoria shook her head.

-I've no idea. There's nothing at all scary in this house or even unusual: no hidden corridors or things that go bump in the night.

-Did she have any friends?

-Yes. Two girlfriends: Rachel and Linda. I don't know their surnames. They were like her though: snobs.

Well, Rachel wasn't too bad; at least she kept the civilities and said hello The three of them met in high school.

-I'd like to talk to them.

The P. I. took out his notepad and wrote the girls' names in it.

-Eddie? Here's a diary…her diary. Should we open it? Here's the key that unlocks the clasp.

He walked over to where his sister stood.

-Let me have it, sis.

He flipped through the pages and noted his sister's slanted handwriting: every page was written in, but the printed dates on each page were crossed out.

-Maybe, later we'll have a real good look at it. Right now, let's go through the rest of the house. You take this floor and I'll look in the attic and take a peek on the rooftop. You never know.

Yolanda found herself alone downstairs. The Latin ice skater didn't appreciate the solitude. She hurried out of the dining room and back into the parlor, looked about the empty room and felt the silence. She glanced out the window and saw the snow coming down. She could hear Edward and Victoria moving about upstairs. How slowly time was passing.

-They're wasting their time. They'll never find her. Catrina's either dead or in hell.

Nella walked in.

-Yolanda? I'm so sorry. I shouldn't have left you alone. No one should be alone now.

She sat down next to Yolanda on the sofa. Nella's pocketbook was still on the floor where she'd left it. She reached into her handbag and took out her compact and applied some powder to her face. She stared into the small mirror. Yolanda was watching her.

-Is that cornsilk powder, Nella? My friend, Dolores, used it, too. She liked it.

-Yes. It's quite nice. I just purchased it the other day at the druggist. Victoria recommended it to me.

Nella felt like screaming at the inanity of this conversation; but, perhaps, it held her sanity together. Perhaps.

-Yes. At the corner drugstore here in Park Slope. The druggist is a good friend of mine. I love going there and just browsing. Somehow, it relaxes me.

-I like doing that, too. It's comforting in a way. It removes you from the pressures of life. And, you always find someone to talk to and, of course, something to buy.

-Yolanda, you're a very lovely girl. My brother is a lucky boy-

They heard footsteps on the stairs. It was Edward and Victoria. The expressions on their faces were blank. Edward spoke to them.

-Nothing. No trace of her. It's as if-

-Did you expect to find her, Edward? She's gone. We'll never see her, again.

-You're probably right, baby; but, we had to try.

Nella touched her brother's arm.

-Of course you did. Edward, mother's in her room with Nathalie. Did you know that she's a practical nurse?

-No. I didn't. But, then again, I don't know anything much about her. How is mother?

-I think she'll be all right. I made her some tea.

-Good. I hope you put a lot of sugar in it.

He gave out an exasperated sigh.

-What is it, Edward? Please, tell us.

-We were given a warning tonight, Victoria. Someone doesn't want us to get too close to the spear. So...that's exactly what we have to do.

He took out a cigarette and lit up.

-Yolanda? Are you up for a midnight run to a Brooklyn cemetery?

-I'm willing to do anything right now. We should have gone there yesterday. -You've been right all along, baby.

-You mean to get the spear, Edward?

-Yes, Nella: to get the damned spear and just maybe save the world. I hope it's not too late.

CHAPTER SEVENTEEN

MARLENA AND Susan found themselves in a large room with no corridors and no foyer. The room took up the entire first floor. There was no furniture except for the ceiling-to-floor bookshelves that lined the four walls of the room. Susan was in awe.

-So many books, mother. It's an impressive collection. I'd love to browse through them all.

-So would I, but not now. And, this is no ordinary room. I can feel an actual pressure emanating from the books themselves. Do you feel it? It's as if we've stepped into a time capsule and all of its contents are alive.

Susan walked over to one book shelf and touched some of the bindings.

-Not a speck of dust and they all look brand new. We must find out who their housekeeper is.

-Susan, keep an eye on that window. We mustn't stay here too long.

The young woman went over to the window that faced the front of the house. There were no blinds or drapes so she stood a little off to the side and out of view from anyone who might be approaching.

Marlena walked the entire circuit of the room. The building was two stories and, yet, there was no staircase to be seen. Perhaps, one of the bookcases hid an upstairs passageway? It would be a daunting task to find it. Did they have time? Marlena looked around. She ran the flashlight along the many shelves of books...every shelf packed solid with them.

The floor. There might be a staircase leading to a cellar. She ran the light along the polished, hardwood floor and saw it: a latch in the form of a metal ring. She yanked hard on it, expecting to open a trap door. Instead, a portion of the bookshelf facing east swung open to reveal a metal, spiral staircase.

-Susan! Look!

Susan ran over to where her mother stood. The spiral staircase not only reached to the second story, but it descended downward, as well. Marlena pointed her flashlight downward, but could see only darkness. The flashlight's beam extended only a few feet and, then, stopped.

-How strange. It looks like some kind of bottomless pit. Here. Take the flashlight, Susan, and point the beam upward.

This time, the flashlight's beam reached to the upper floor.

-I'm going upstairs to investigate. Give me the flash-light back. Stay down here and keep your eyes peeled to that window. I have an uneasy feeling about this place.

Susan reached into her trench coat pocket and took out a small, pen light.

-I'll point the beam upward if I see anyone coming.

Marlena started up the stairs.

Susan was now left alone. She went over to the book-shelves and ran her penlight's beam over some of the titles. The books weren't in any kind of order. The titles were interesting: The Origin of Sumer, The Great Begin-ning, Immortality and the Strain Upon Man, Infin-ity…and more. She had to force herself away from the books. She knew that they were in danger and that her mother was depending on her as a lookout. The young woman walked back over to the front window holding on to the book entitled "Infinity."

Marlena was on to the second floor and couldn't quite make out what she was seeing. She played the flashlight's beam around the room and saw nothing: no books, no furniture….nothing except a black geometric shape on the floor. It was a circle, but it contained noth-ing. The circle was pitch black. Marlena walked toward it.

-Is it solid? It must be.

She stepped closer to its edge. The flashlight's beam did not show a black surface. The light was lost in the pitch blackness.

-The light is being absorbed like some kind of a black sponge. It's not solid. What in the world can it be?

An object was floating to the surface of the black circle. It was human...or had once been human. A head emerged and Marlena stifled a gasp. It was the naked body of a woman...horribly scarred. Marlena backed away. She saw the face of the woman, but had no way of knowing that it was Catrina Mendez.

Downstairs, Susan was flipping through her book, "Infinity." The texture of the pages was different from the many books that she had read. The pages were thinner and with a different style of print. The jacket was muted and soft like satin.

Remembering her assignment, she peered out the window, but saw no sign of anyone approaching. The snow was still coming down and this made visibility easier in the new darkness that had settled on to the planet. Telling herself that all was clear, she went back to the book in her hand.

-Susan? Susan!

She ran over to the spiral staircase.

-What is it?

-Flash you pen's beam on to the corner of the ceiling. Hurry!

Susan ran over to the corner and did as her mother asked. All the young woman could make out was a blank, white ceiling. She ran back to the staircase.

-There's nothing there but the ceiling. What should I be seeing?

-I'm coming down.

She heard her mother's heavy footsteps.

-Well?

-There's a body up there that's been horribly burned.

-My God! Who is it? Who *was* it?

-A woman. I'd say that it was radiation burns.

Susan looked about the room while trying to take this information in.

-Could she still be alive?

-I doubt it. I didn't examine the body, though. It was suspended in some kind of black tunnel. If she is alive, she'd be better off dead.

-Shouldn't we help her?

-No. We can't risk it. And, besides, that black circle that she's in…I think it would be dangerous to get too close to it.

-Mother, let's leave this place. It gives me the creeps.

-Not yet. What are you reading?

Susan showed her the book.

-Go back to the window and stay there.

-What are you going to do?

-Search for any books on the spear. There must be something here.

-I'll help and still be a lookout.

-I know how you are with books, young lady.

-I won't be distracted.

-Don't. I mean it. Our lives may depend on it.

Marlena was about to run her flashlight's beam over the many books when she felt it. The air in the room was clean and cool, but not cold. The inside temperature was perfect. She could have easily taken off her trench coat. Everything in the house felt wrong. It felt fake. The only thing that felt real or of any substance had been the spiral staircase.

Susan had another book in her hands and this time she noted something quite interesting. She turned away from the window and just missed seeing a point of moving light in the distance.

-Mother, look at this.

She ran over to the opposite side of the room to show her mother her extraordinary find.

-Look at the copyright date: 1989; that's forty-two years into the future. That would explain the different texture and style of the book.

Marlena looked at the copyright date and grabbed another book off the shelf. She flipped to the copyright page and it read: 1975. It was a book by a Dr. Carl Sagan. She had to see more.

Susan ran back to the window and this time she saw that point of light approaching.

-Mother, someone is coming!

-Not now. I must see more.

Susan turned back to the window and saw two points of light in the near distance.

Marlena was scanning the bookshelves like a madwoman. She pulled out a volume by an Arthur C. Clarke. She read the copyright date: 1969. She held on to it. She next chose a volume on Parallel Universes by a Dr. Bennett Matsui: copyright date: 2023.

-Mother! There are people coming.

-What? Oh! How far away are they?

-About a hundred yards, maybe less. We've got to leave now.

-Just one more volume. I've simply got to see more.

-Hurry up for heaven's sake.

The two figures were moving directly toward the house. How could they possibly get out unseen?

Marlena grabbed one more volume: WW III by Professor Barnett Schumann: copyright date: 2093.

Susan ran over to where her mother was.

-It's too late. We can't get out now. They'll see us.

-Where are they? Show me.

They turned off their flashlights and went over to the window. The two figures were about to climb the front stairs.

-We waited too long.

-Shut up and listen to me. Go and crouch down in the far corner while I try and close that bookshelf. Hurry!

Susan ran to the far corner of the room. Her mother found the key ring in the floor and yanked hard on it. The bookshelf swung shut. She ran over to join her daughter just as the front door opened.

-Keep your fingers crossed and get ready to fight for your life.

Susan didn't answer her, but a horrible thought just flashed through her head: would they be able to detect the perfume that she was wearing? She didn't voice this concern to her mother. What would be the point? If they were spotted, it could mean the end. She noticed that her mother was holding on to several books. Susan held on to her own book.

A man and a woman walked in. The two women in the corner watched the new arrivals. The woman walked over to where the latch was. She bent down to pull it. Susan had to stifle a gasp. It was the same middle-aged woman who had chased her down 5th Ave. the other day. Susan could only assume that her companion was the same man. She glanced at her mother crouching in the dark. Her mother's hand was inside her pocketbook holding on to her gun.

The middle-aged woman had now opened the secret door. She and her male companion went over to the opening and climbed up the spiral staircase.

Marlena stage whispered to her daughter.

-Let's get the hell out of here!

They got to their feet and went straight to the front door, opened it and fled down the wooden steps and into the night.

-Whatever you do, Susan, don't look back.

Susan heeded her mother's advice and it was a good thing that she did. The two people who were now on the second floor of the house that they'd just fled from had spotted the two women in flight. They hesitated for just a moment before they ran down the spiral staircase in pursuit. But, Marlena and Susan had a head start and were already nearing their car. They got in and slammed shut the doors and locked them…but, the car wouldn't start.

-What's wrong? Why won't it start? Answer me, young lady.

-I think I'm flooding the engine. Wait just a second- Oh!

Susan saw two beams of light coming from the direction of the house.

-What is it? They spotted us! Susan, try to start it, again, but go easy on the accelerator. Hurry! They're getting closer.

Susan Broder was not the panicky type, but she was coming close to desperation. Marlena took her gun out of her pocketbook and aimed it at the two beams of approaching light. She fired a shot at one and, then, fired a second shot at the other. The two beams of light wavered and spun, but quickly righted themselves and continued forward.

Susan put the key back in the ignition and managed to turn over the engine.

-Thank God!

-Now, step on it. If they catch up to us, they'll kill us with no questions asked.

Susan floored the gas pedal and made a sweeping U-turn back on to the main highway. They made good their escape.

CHAPTER EIGHTEEN

IT WAS late at night when Edward and Yolanda made their way from Mrs. Mendez's house and into the snow storm. Edward was wearing an old pair of snow boots and Yolanda had borrowed Victoria's. They had to wait for Nathalie. She'd been with Mrs. Mendez, calming the old woman down. The Frenchwoman was in the back seat now and lighting herself a cigarette.

-Your mother was recovering quite nicely, cherie. She is strong.

Edward nodded in agreement, keeping his eye on the road.

-We'll have to drive out to the edge of the cemetery and park across the street. I know where the mausoleum is. At least, I think I remember where it is. I don't go there too often. In a way, it'll be a lot easier to break in than to dig up six feet of earth.

-I agree, cherie. So much neater and simpler and with less complication.

-The snow's easing up, so we won't have to trudge through a lot of snow drifts.

-Dear Miss Estravades, that is true; but, it feels much colder than it did a few hours ago. The planet's temperature must be dropping, no? I cannot bear to even think about it.

Edward and Yolanda had to agree with their backseat passenger. The inside of the car felt like a butcher's freezer and even with the heater on every piece of metal was ice cold. It was a good thing that Edward had brought along some steamer blankets and these they spread over their legs for some measure of warmth.

There were no cars on the street, not at this hour: the quiet and utter darkness of the night was unnerving. The falling snow cast specters of light over the street lamps' round, glass orbs causing blurred illuminations through their glass prisms. Were they the only moving vehicle in the entire city? Edward laughed out loud at that thought. Any moment now and they'd probably run into a squad car.

-Is it a long ride, Edward?

-It's not much further. We'll be there in about twenty minutes or so and, then, the fun really begins. Nervous, baby?

-A little…maybe more.

-It'll keep you on your toes. My own feet are freezing.

-My mother once told me that walking in the snow heats you up.

-My mother told me that once, too.

Edward glanced toward the back-seat.

-How you holding up back there, Nathalie?

-Not bad. And, this back-seat is quite comfortable: one could almost lay back and fall asleep.

And, in about twenty minutes…

-Yolanda. Nathalie. There it is: Highland Park Cemetery. It's right next to Highland Park. On a clear day, the view's pretty spectacular; it lives up to its name. I'll try to park as close as I can to the entrance. Keep a sharp lookout.

Edward parked his car in front of an apartment building where no lights were showing in any of the windows. The three people climbed out of the car and walked across the street and into the cemetery. Edward kept a sharp lookout for the mausoleum and for anyone else who they might encounter. His right hand kept reaching for his gun holster: a good reflex action. He couldn't help but notice that there were so many stone structures used to accommodate so many rotting corpses: such a waste of manpower and material to build them. He shone his flashlight over the door of each mausoleum just to make sure he didn't pass the right one.

-Can't take any chances. Not now. And, it has been awhile since I've been here.

Yolanda was about to answer her boyfriend when she felt the ground tremble beneath her feet. It was a minor tremor and it lasted for no longer than a few moments, but it terrified her.

-Edward, did you feel that?

It was Nathalie who responded.

-An earth tremor. Are they very common in this region?

It was Edward's turn to answer.

-No. Most of New York City is built on bedrock. What we just felt...

Yolanda wouldn't let him off with a dangling sentence.

-What did we feel? That was no ordinary earthquake, I bet.

-It might have been a planetary tremor; something that the entire planet felt.

Yolanda understood.

-Edward, that could mean that the Earth is moving out of its orbit. If it does, it won't matter if the sun reappears or not.

-It ain't easy, baby, but try not to think about it. It didn't last long and the tremor was slight. And, if you're gonna' pray, then pray real hard we don't get another one.

Without warning, he grabbed Yolanda's arm.

-There it is! It's right in front of us — the mausoleum.

He ran up to the iron door and played the flashlight's beam on to the engraved stone.

-My father's resting place.

Edward, Yolanda, and Nathalie climbed the five stone steps. The wrought iron door was open.

-What the hell is this? Who's been here?

-The caretaker could have left it open, cherie. They can be careless. After all, what is there to steal?

-I hope you're right about that for all our sakes.

Edward swung open the iron gate. The oak door behind it was locked.

-Looks like you were right, Nathalie. Now, to break in.

The P. I. took out a thin piece of metal, not unlike the one Marlena had used, and slipped it into the door's bolt. He turned it left and, then, right. The lock snapped open.

Yolanda smiled with approval at him.

-You'd make a good cat burglar, Edward. We could even go to Paris and live on the Left Bank with our ill-gotten gain.

-Don't tempt me, baby.

Before opening the door, they shook their coats free of snow. Edward opened the door and went inside. He flashed the beam of light in all directions to penetrate the darkness. He walked the full length of the mausoleum. His father's coffin was the only thing in the room and it was at the center. Yolanda and Nathalie stayed near the door.

-Yolanda? Close the door, will you? No sense in letting the cold air in.

She did. And, she also noticed how warm and downright pleasant it was in the mausoleum.

-Edward? The air is so nice and fresh. I thought it would be cold and damp.

-Mon Dieu! It *is* quite nice in here. I wonder...

The P. I. looked over his shoulder.

-We can wonder about a lot of things later.

Nathalie cast Yolanda a significant glance.

-He comes straight to the purpose, your boyfriend.

Edward put down his mason's bag and took out a crowbar.

-I need elbow room. Yolanda, hold my flashlight, will you?

Yolanda and Nathalie moved to the other side of the coffin as Edward began his unnerving task. He placed the crowbar under the lid of the casket and began prying it open. At first, the lid wouldn't budge.

-Harder, cherie, harder.

They heard a creak. The lid began to open.

Edward straightened up.

-There. I can do it by hand, now.

He hesitated. Yolanda came around to his side of the coffin.

-Just do it quickly, Edward. It's the only way.

-Listen to her, cherie. Do it, for pity's sake. Put your fear aside. A corpse cannot hurt you.

Edward braced himself and flung open the lid of the dead man's coffin.

Nathalie came around the coffin to join Edward and Yolanda. The Frenchwoman screamed. What lay inside the coffin was the outline of a man's figure that had deteriorated to dust. Beside the dust was the Spear of Longinus. Its length was six feet and it was made of what looked like polished, dark wood. On the end of its shaft was a point of gleaming metal that was razor sharp and glowed a muted green. Edward thought he heard a humming noise emanating from it. He could feel its vibration: a storehouse of energy that was limitless and dangerous.

The P. I. turned away to get the gloves he'd brought with him. They were lead-lined gloves that his father had used. Edward's mother had told him where they were: in the cellar of the house. As he bent down to take them out of the mason bag, Yolanda cried out.

-Edward! Nathalie is taking the spear.

Yolanda tried to stop her, but Nathalie drew a pistol on her. By this time, Edward had straightened up and was reaching for his gun.

-No, cherie, put away your weapon. It is I who have the spear and a gun, as well, and it is pointed directly at your girlfriend.

-I knew we couldn't trust this bitch, Edward.

-Call me whatever you like. It doesn't matter. My friends are coming and that is most unfortunate for the two of you.

-Why, Nathalie? Who are your friends? Your fellow Nazis?

-Such questions! Why should I tell you anything? All my life I have waited for this moment. I was denied it once. I will not be denied it, again.

-You want to help destroy a planet? To kill three billion people and every living creature on it? You and your kind are nothing but filth: traitors to humanity.

-I don't deny it, Mr. Mendez; but, we will survive and that is all that counts. My only regret is that Werner Hoffman is not here to revel in the moment.

Yolanda looked at Edward. She moved her hand to get a tighter hold on her purse and in one quick gesture, she flung it hard into Nathalie's face. The Frenchwoman's gun went off, but it missed its target with the bullet ricocheting off the stone wall. Edward knocked Nathalie down and the spear rolled across the mausoleum's floor. He put his gloves on and picked up the spear.

Nathalie recovered and ran out into the night. Yolanda was about to go after her when Edward stopped her.

-Let her go. We've got what we came for. And, I've got the car keys. She won't get too far.

Nathalie had run only a short distance when something in the snow made her stop. A black circle appeared on the ground only a few feet away from her. It grew in diameter. The light snow falling into it disappeared into an inky black chasm.

Nathalie screamed and turned to run when another tremor struck: this one was more violent than the first and lasted longer. She was thrown to the ground away from the black disc. She recovered and kept her wits about her. Without hesitation, she ran further into the cemetery: better to take her chances in an unknown area than to face that black abyss of hell. She knew that once again her so-called allies had betrayed her. She was on her own…but maybe not quite.

Two figures emerged from the black circle and walked toward the mausoleum.

-Edward, did you hear that? It sounded like a woman's scream.

-It sounded like Nathalie.

He almost lost his balance.

-And, that was another earth tremor. Let's get the hell out of here. Whatever got her is probably coming for us.

Edward slammed down the lid of his father's coffin. He and his girlfriend made for the door but stopped short when they saw the two figures approaching.

-Oh, my God! Who are they?

-Enemies, baby.

He put the spear down and drew his gun. He shouted into the night.

-Get the hell back or I shoot.

The two figures did not stop.

Edward aimed for the one on the right. His bullet went right through it. This time, he tried shooting it in the head. It staggered back, but kept moving.

-Yolanda, get behind me.

He tried slamming the door shut, but it stuck mid-way.

-My God, Edward, hurry!

The two figures were now climbing the mausoleum steps and still Edward couldn't get the door shut.

Yolanda shouted to her boyfriend.

-Pull away from the door for a second. That's it! Now, push it shut.

Edward, putting all his weight and strength behind it, slammed the door shut just as the two figures reached the top step.

-Man, that was too close for comfort, baby.

The P. I. wiped the sweat from his brow.

-We're not of it yet. Look!

-Get back.

The two of them moved away from the door as the two figures outside started pounding on it.

-Edward, they'll break it down.

The P. I. picked up the spear.

-Maybe this will stop them.

The door burst open. Edward pointed the spear at the intruders. Instinct told him to.

-Yolanda, close your eyes!

He closed his eyes, as well

The metallic point of the spear emitted a blinding, green light. It hit the figure on the left and and, then, the one on the right. The green light shot back into the spear.

Edward approached the door as Yolanda opened her eyes. He saw two melted heaps of metal and plastic on the floor.

-What were they, Edward? Not human. They couldn't be.

-Robots or androids, most likely. Don't get too close. I can feel the heat still coming out of them.

He measured the weight of the spear with his grip and smiled with satisfaction.

-Like something out of an H. G. Wells novel, huh? Not bad.

-Only this is all too real and frightening.

-We don't have time to wonder about it now. Let's head for Marlena's place. We got what we came for. And, at least, we know this baby works.

CHAPTER NINETEEN

AS EDWARD and Yolanda emerged from the mausoleum, the black hole vanished without a trace. The couple made their way back to Edward's car. Yolanda was holding on to the empty canvas bag. Edward had the spear. When they neared the Ford, they noticed a squad car parked behind it. Lt. Donovan waved to them.

-Miss Estravades? Mendez?

Edward waved back.

-Glad to see you, Lieutenant. How did you know where to find us?

-Your sister, Nella, spilled the beans.

-Is she and my sister, Victoria, and my mother okay?

-They're being guarded. Don't worry.

-It's a bad habit I've got.

-Is that the spear?

-It is. And, have we got a story to tell you.

-Why don't you and Miss Estravades get in your car and follow me into the city? We can park that spear at the precinct. And, I've got some news of my own for the two of you.

Yolanda smiled coyly.

-Oh? Good news for a change, Lieutenant?

-Depends on how you look at it, Miss Estravades. Hoffman, Sr. tried hanging himself in his cell-

-Oh, my God!

-and, we had to let Holderman go and not that we wanted to.

Edward shook his head.

-You shouldn't have. He'll try and make a run for it.

-We know where to find him; and, I put a tail on him just in case.

Everyone climbed into their respective cars and headed toward Manhattan. The snow had stopped, but the wind had picked up and it was brutal.

-Edward?

-What is it, baby? Light me a cigarette for me, will you?

She lit two cigarettes, handed one to him and, then, asked her question.

-Now, that we have the spear, what do we do with it?

-I'll just tell you my gut instinct: we point it to where the sun oughta' be.

-That makes a lot of sense. But, how do we know where and when to point it?

-I've been thinking about that.

-Oh? I knew that I had a smart boyfriend.

-We need to get a hold of an astronomer. What about your Professor Lange? He'd know where to point the damned thing.

-He should be easy to reach; that is, if Marlena hasn't frightened him off. He's a public figure. He works for the Hayden Planetarium.

-If we can't reach him, we could always try for his secretary. And- of course! What about Susan? She's brainy enough.

-She might be able to help; but, I bet Professor Lange would know for sure where to point the spear.

-Maybe, we'll corral the two of them. They should make quite a team. Here's the turn-off. We'll be in the city soon.

The squad car and Edward's car were parked just outside of the 86th precinct. Every light in the building was on because every available police officer was on duty. Upstairs on the third floor, Edward, Yolanda, Lt. Donovan, and Sgt. Rayno were in conference. The bitterly cold wind was still howling outside.

-Did Hoffman leave any note?

-No.

-Will he live?

-It's touch-and-go. We cut him down just in time.

There was a minute of silence in the cold room before Lt. Donovan picked up the conversation.

-Well, what now? And, what about these Nazis? A couple of my men are tracking down this Ricardo Montenegro.

Edward leaned back in his chair and took a long drag on his cigarette.

-The Nazis have some pretty strange weapons. They get around through a sort of black hole device, I think. It's like a portal through time and space. And, they know how to make androids...pretty deadly androids.

-But, where's their home base? If we knew that, we could disable them.

Yolanda addressed the Lieutenant.

-Antarctica: that's what Professor Lange told Marlena. I think this black hole they use is their only method of travel. I don't think that they can use it themselves; that's why they send androids through. This black hole kills or injures people because of the radiation. We saw that happen to Edward's sister, Catrina, tonight. I'll bet these surviving Nazis are trapped in their own home base at the bottom of the world.

Sgt. Rayno spoke up.

-So, only these homemade robots can get through? This sounds like science fiction magazine stuff.

-I wish it were fiction, Sergeant, but like Yolanda just said, we've seen it with our own eyes. The question is: how the hell did they get a hold of this kind of equipment? Yolanda, you're the expert on this.

-I wish! But, I think it's part science and part occult science. A lot of Nazis were practiced occultists, you know. Hitler, himself, was obsessed with it. I was even told that it eventually drove him insane.

Lt. Donovan shook his head in frustration.

-I'm with Sergeant Rayno on this. How did they come up with all this science fiction stuff?

The door opened and Professor Lange walked in. He took off his overcoat and hat and sat down. He was breathing heavily.

-I'll answer your question, Lieutenant.: from an ancient but advanced civilization. The Nazi expeditions to the Antarctic paid off. They must have discovered the remnants of a long forgotten civilization.

Lt. Donovan nodded and offered the professor a cigarette which he accepted.

-Please, continue, Professor Lange. We're listening.

-I'm afraid I don't know much more than that.

Lt. Donovan grinned.

-How do you know that much? And, try catching your breath.

-I was privy to military reports during the last war. I worked with the Air Force on several top secret projects. They needed my expertise in astronomy.

Edward asked the question that had been on his mind for a couple of days now.

-Professor Lange, just how did the Nazis know to even go to Antarctica? Who tipped them off?

-That's the million dollar question, isn't it, Mr. Mendez? Through their dabbling in the occult? Through some kind of contact with an extraterrestrial race who visited the Earth? Don't laugh, Sergeant Rayno. We have evidence that extraterrestrial beings landed on this planet at least once before in the distant past. Or, perhaps, they went down there for strategic purposes of launching more advanced V2 rockets? Who knows what they were up to?

Edward thought back to the photographs in his office: the photos of the atomic bomb testings and the white "specks" and "folds." He looked at the professor and decided that he didn't trust him. In spite of this, he blurted out his next sentence to see this man's reaction.

-We have the spear, Professor.

It took Professor Lange a moment to react.

-The spear of Longinus. Yes. It could be heavily radioactive, Mr. Mendez. It could even contain some form of magnetic radiation. You were careful in handling it, I trust.

-How did you know that I'd handled it?

-I didn't.

-To answer your question, I was as careful as I could be. Now, Professor Lange, do we point it at the sun? Will that bring back the daylight?

Professor Lange put out his cigarette.

-I'll give a cautious "yes" to that question. It *should* work.

Edward had to gather his thoughts to pose his next question. He was aware that all eyes in the small conference room were on him. He took a deep drag on his cigarette, leaned back in his chair and let out a stream of smoke toward the ceiling. The sound of the gale force wind outside got his attention. How much worse would *that* get? He glanced at his girlfriend and smiled.

-Professor, when and where do we deploy our new weapon?

The P. I. couldn't have made his question any more straightforward.

-You're a man, Mr. Mendez, who comes straight to the point. I like that. You'd make a good scientist. In two days: on the 18th of December. Past that date, and the atmosphere may begin to liquify. The temperature is expected to drop dramatically within the next seventy-two hours. And, the planet tremors have already begun. The Earth is starting to shift in its orbit. We've less time than we thought.

Sgt. Rayno gave out a nervous laugh.

-Thanks for the pep talk, Professor!

Lt Donovan interrupted.

-Can we wait two days, Professor? The weather out there is getting colder by the hour. And, who knows when the next earth tremor will hit.

-As I was about to say, Lieutenant: it must be the day after tomorrow. I'll need that much time to get the exact space coordinates. Where? At first, I considered aiming it from atop the Empire State Building, but maneuvering the spear there would be dangerous in such a populated area as midtown Manhattan. If we're dealing with magnetic radiation, the entire city could be contaminated by the fallout from the spear.

Lt. Donovan leaned forward in his chair. He took a cigarette out of a nearly empty pack.

-Then, where, God damn it? We need to know now, so we can set things up. Don't play cozy with us, Professor.

-The Statue of Liberty: it's isolated and we can maneuver the spear from atop the torch. I'll need to go there as soon as possible to check the exact coordinates and time. I could go there tonight.

-Sgt. Rayno will get you there.

-I'll have to get some instruments back at my office. And, I'll need my secretary's help, if that's all right.

-You'll get whatever you need. Sgt. Rayno will take you along with however many men I can spare. What is it, Professor Lange. You look worried.

-Only to say that we're all in great danger. These Nazis have gotten their hands on technology that I'm not even sure they can control.

Edward addressed the Lieutenant.

-You better tell your men to bring all the hardware and artillery they can lay their hands on. We're gonna' need it in a couple of days.

-Like what?

-Hand grenades. Machine guns. I got this real gut feeling that we're in for a battle.

Nathalie Montaigne stopped to rest. She was cold and exhausted and angry with herself. She'd been a fool to act so hastily back there at the mausoleum, but what else could she have done? Time was the enemy to everyone now. A risk had to be taken and she had taken it and failed.

Nathalie leaned against a tombstone and knew that she had to take immediate action to save her life. Mendez had the spear and now she would pray to all the saints that he would save the world. She knew that her former allies would not forgive her failure and that was too damned bad for them; always leaving the dirty work for others. Let them all rot in hell where they so deserved to be.

With a shiver running down her spine, Nathalie straightened up and started back to the main avenue. She must find shelter for the night, a hotel would have to do; but, first, she had to reach a phone and make an urgent call and, then, somehow get back to the anonymity of the city.

And, after a much difficult walk, she found herself on Fulton St., a main thoroughfare, and…yes…there was an elevated train station on the corner. She spotted a phone booth right by the train's stairwell and hurried toward it. She got in and closed the accordion door. At least she was out of that dreadful wind. She dropped a coin in the phone's slot. The line on the other side started to ring.

-Answer, damn it! You must be there. Dearest Savior-

-Hello?

-It is I, Nathalie. Listen carefully, for I have no time to repeat myself.

-Go ahead.

-Mendez has the spear. If he has not been stopped, he is surely on his way to the police with the trophy. An earth tremor hit as I was fleeing for my life. I will look after myself. Do you understand?

-Yes.

The line clicked at the other end and Nathalie hung up the phone.

-There! Now, they can do as they please. But, Mr. Mendez, Nathalie is rooting for your success. Yes. I am a pragmatist who wants to live.

Nathalie climbed the stairwell leading to the token booth. She heard voices up ahead and was surprised to see so many people gathered in the small waiting area. A disturbance must have occurred. She opened the door and walked in, purchased her token, and went through the wooden turnstile. There were about a good dozen people looking out on to the platform. Nathalie was not shy about asking questions. She approached a group of people who were obviously traveling together: they consisted of a woman and two young boys and two teenage girls.

She addressed the woman.

-Do you know what is going on? Are the trains not running?

-There was a terrible accident just a few minutes ago: a man fell in front of a train. The police are out there now on the platform.

Nathalie was taken aback.

-Mon Dieu! How terrible. He is dead, of course.

The woman nodded her head.

-They're taking him off the tracks…what's left of him. We're just coming back from my daughter's high school dance revue. What a lousy way to end an evening.

-How charming. Life does go on. Are these all your children?

-Oh, no. The younger girl is my daughter and the other girl is a friend of the family.

Nathalie noted that the daughter had a Parisienne quality to her: the good bone structure and the clear, porcelain-like complexion.

-But, are you of French extract? Your daughter is clearly-

Before Nathalie could finish her question, the outer door exiting on to the platform opened up and two police officers came through holding open the door for the stretcher. A white sheet covered the body, but the face had not been completely hidden and what had once been a human hand was also exposed: one could just make out the blood and mutilated flesh of the victim. There were gasps among the crowd and a young, black girl almost fainted.

In a moment, the spectacle was over. In the near distance, Nathalie could hear an approaching train. Thank God! Within the hour, she would check into the Waldorf Astoria: it was quite a huge hotel and she could afford to stay for a few days, at least. Werner Hoffman had been generous with his money and she was most grateful for it now.

Nathalie and the other passengers walked out on to the platform to await the train's arrival. The wind had picked up and the crystalline snow was like particles of glass. Nathalie, again, addressed the woman. Her curiosity got the best of her.

-Was it a suicide? You don't think there was foul play involved?

The woman shrugged her shoulders.

-Who knows? What the hell was he doing out on that platform in this weather and in all this blackness? He should have stayed in the waiting area with the rest of us. If you ask me, he was up to no good.

-Was there anyone else on the platform with him? Were there any witnesses? It could prove to be important.

-I'm not sure. I really didn't notice, but there might have been.

The younger of the two boys spoke up. He was wearing wire rimmed spectacles and was eager to join in the conversation with the adults.

-He *was* with another man. I saw the both of them go outside; but, I don't think they were friends. The other man was scared. His friend came back in with the police, I think.

-That is most interesting, young man. You are observant.

Nathalie made the sign of the cross.

-May God have mercy on his soul.

Why did the incident disturb her so? It involved total strangers who had in no way entered into her sphere of life. And, besides, she had problems of her own.

The train pulled into the station and Nathalie got on with the rest of the commuters. She found a seat in the corner of the car. Good. Now, she could begin to make her plans. She opened her purse to check its contents. Yes. All her money was still there and it was enough to see her through the next few weeks. Nathalie thought of her old friend, Werner Hoffman, with affection: a good man and hopefully he will survive. He was now in police custody, true, but on what charge could they possibly hold him? He had committed no crime. And what about Holderman? He had committed many crimes, but which one could they prosecute him on? With his luck, he'd probably be set free. Bastard! She had never liked him: a dyed in the wool Nazi if ever there had been one.

The train sped on through the inky blackness and was making all its appointed stops. The car was emptying out and the woman and her entourage got off at the transfer point that would take them further into Brooklyn leaving Nathalie and another woman by themselves in the car. The Frenchwoman had no way of knowing that she would once again meet the woman and her family under most unusual and horrific circumstances.

Nathalie's "companion" in the train car was not watching her. She saw this, took out her compact and studied her face. She had on far too much make-up and her wig was now slightly askew. With an adept hand, she took the wig off and placed it next to her on the "straw" seat. Then, with a small cosmetic sponge, she wiped off the rouge and mascara. Good. The lipstick she didn't entirely erase; a trace of red would remain so as not to look too conspicuous.

She put the cosmetic sponge next to the wig; both would be disposed of as soon as she got off. The train was now crossing the Williamsburg bridge into Manhattan. Nathalie stood up to look at her handiwork in the reflection of one of the car windows. She gasped at the sight.

-Mon Dieu! How old and tired I look! So dreadful to see oneself in such unflattering terms. Enough.

Her salt and pepper hair was arranged in a chignon and her complexion looked pale and lined. Nathalie looked away from the image. She took a blue, silk scarf from her bag and put it on. It didn't help much; but, she took solace in the fact that no one would ever recognize her now; except, perhaps, for Mendez's girlfriend, Yolanda. That little bitch was sharp...too sharp for her own good. Perhaps, one day, their paths would once again cross.

CHAPTER TWENTY

EDWARD AND Yolanda drove over to Marlena's place. The spear had been placed in a lead container in a cell at the precinct and it was under twenty-four hour guard and no one without the proper authorization was allowed to go anywhere near it. Yolanda had not wanted to leave it there. It was against her better judgement. She was annoyed with her boyfriend.

-Edward, we should have kept it close to us. It's yours, you know. It's part of your inheritance from your father.

-It'll be safe enough. And, besides, we'll be getting it back day after tomorrow; that is, if we succeed.

-I suppose that you're right; but, I still feel uneasy about it. We took the risk in getting it. We should have it and not that police detective.

-Here's Marlena's place.

The P. I. pulled up just a few feet from the brownstone before he cut the car's engine. He and his girlfriend walked up to the front door and rang the bell. The wind brought tears to their eyes and the ice crystals stung their faces. Edward had to hold on to his hat.

Susan answered the door.

-We've been waiting for you. Did everything go all right?

Susan didn't wait for an answer. She led the way into the living room where her mother was pouring coffee for them. Edward stopped off in the corridor to phone his sister, Nella, and to hang up his wet overcoat and hat. Marlena called out from the living room.

-Edward? Yolanda? Susan just made us all some java.

-Just making a fast phone call, Marlena.

Edward completed his call and made his way into the, as usual, dark living room. Yolanda was standing in the doorway waiting for him, still dressed to go out.

-We've much to tell you. By the way, dear boy, did you get the spear?

Edward laughed: same old Marlena with the cavalier attitude. He took off his suit jacket and helped Yolanda off with her overcoat. He whispered to his girlfriend.

-We're not going out again, relax. And, put your purse down. Okay?

He kissed her on the cheek.

The coffee was served and the ensuing conversation took several hours that lasted into the morning.

-So, Edward, you will be the one to focus the spear. It must be you and no one else. It's a pity that you didn't actually contact your father. He might have told us a great deal. I'd like to know more about that enigmatic man. He died carrying many secrets to his grave, I'm sure. Did he leave any journals or diaries behind? I'd like to get my hands on them.

Edward sat back on the sofa and put his arm around Yolanda. He could still sense her anger.

-I don't know. My mother would know; but, I doubt if she'd share any personal journals.

-If your father was an occultist worth his salt, he would have kept at least one magical journal.

-From what I've been told, he was a pretty methodical man. I'll ask around. I'd like to have a look at them myself, but don't get your hopes up too high.

-And, as to this Professor Lange, I don't trust him. He tells only what is to his advantage.

Yolanda had to smile at this last statement of Marlena's. Her annoyance with Edward was beginning to slip away.

-Marlena, we agree. This is a great day. I'm not so sure that I trust the professor either. His answers are too clipped…it's like someone had slipped him the answers to an examination.

Susan spoke up.

-It looks like none of us trusts the good professor and that's something worth thinking about.

Edward turned to Yolanda and put his arm around her waist.

-And, baby, it looks like someone did slip him the questions *and* the answers.

Marlena put down her coffee cup.

-Good. Of course, Susan will also check for the proper coordinates as to where exactly the earth will be in relation to the sun. I do trust my own daughter implicitly. We can rely on her.

Susan held up her cup of coffee for a mock toast.

-Why thank you, mother.

-Susan, show Edward and Yolanda the books we appropriated from that so-called Lodge. It was quite a find.

Susan put down her coffee cup and left the room to get them.

-Marlena, you said that the house didn't have a speck of dust in it.

-Quite extraordinary. I didn't know what to make of it.

-That book shop of Holderman's was in the same kind of pristine condition. It just doesn't make sense. And, come to think of it, so was Catrina's room back in Brooklyn.

Marlena finished her coffee.

-The cops shouldn't have released Holderman. He must be involved in this up to his scrawny neck. He might have given us some vital information. But, his book shop and that Lodge...both storehouses that are kept in controlled climates...probably to preserve the books' integrity. But why? *Why*? And, what was the purpose of your father's Lodge?

Susan came back with the four books. She gave two of them to Edward and the other two to Yolanda.

-Edward? Yolanda? Look at the copyright dates. It's extraordinary.

Edward stared at the copyright page.

-2023, but-

Marlena interrupted him.

-That date does not mean that we will be successful. Don't be misled.

-How do you figure that, Marlena? If this is from the future-

-These books, Edward, could come from a parallel time: a parallel earth. They could even be fictitious.

The P. I. shook his head.

-I don't think so. And, the more I think about it, the more certain I am that my father wasn't your run-of-the-mill occultist either. I'd like to know where *he* came from.

-Those books might have been placed there to give us false confidence. It would be a very cunning diversion tactic. It's been done before.

Edward was forced to agree.

-Maybe. These creeps are pretty clever. You might just be right about that diversion bit.

Susan addressed Edward.

-When will Professor Lange be ready, Edward. Did he say? He must have.

-Sometime today, I think. He's supposed to get in touch with Lt. Donovan who'll get in touch with me. He made a run out to the Statue of Liberty with Sgt. Rayno. He was pretty anxious to get there.

Marlena grinned at that last statement.

-We've no time to waste. Susan, go upstairs and see what you can come up with. The books that I had you take out from the library the other day should help. I'll clean up down here. Call me if you need me.

Susan finished her coffee and went upstairs to her room. Marlena turned to face Edward.

-You should have brought the spear back here. Why didn't you? It's yours. Can we trust this Lt. Donovan? I don't like him.

Yolanda laughed and helped herself to another cup of coffee.

-Marlena, we agree twice in one day. What kind of an omen can that be?

Edward took out a cigarette and lit up.

-Lt. Donovan's honest. I'd stake my life on that. We couldn't chance bringing it here because Yolanda and I might have been waylaid en route. And, besides, that spear is pretty "hot," if you get my meaning.

Marlena wasn't convinced.

-Don't worry, you'll see the spear soon enough. You *are* coming with us, Marlena?

-Of course, dear boy. I wouldn't miss it for the world. It'll be fun.

Marlena was in the kitchen cleaning up. Yolanda had gone upstairs to rest and to make a phone call to her coach. Susan was doing her usual research. Good. The P. I. needed this time to himself.

How many days had it been? How many days since it had all started? Four days. Yes. Four action-packed, God-awful days.

Edward looked at his watch: 10 A.M. Where was Wulf Holderman? If he were anywhere, he'd be at his book shop or just maybe at that house where Marlena and Susan had visited last night.

And, then…he felt another earth tremor: not severe but this one lasted a couple of minutes. He was about to get up when Marlena came into the living room carrying a tray.

-Edward, let's go into the dining room for a few minutes. I've just warmed up some bacon and eggs and there's juice and coffee. You must eat.

A couple of minutes later, Edward was enjoying his breakfast in the dining room with his erstwhile hostess.

-I assume you felt that earth tremor a few minutes ago? Quite unnerving.

-I couldn't not feel it. They're getting longer.

-The planet is trying to maintain its orbit. You might say that it's fighting to stay in place. At least, that's how Susan explained it.

-I hope it wins the fight. But, Marlena, I've been wondering about something.

-Yes?

Edward smiled and pointed his slice of bacon at her.

-Where do *you* fit into all of this?

-I don't quite get your drift.

-You know more than you're telling.

-I make it my business to be well informed. It's my insatiable curiosity.

Marlena helped herself to another strip of bacon.

-Edward, that house in Staten Island...something just occurred to me. It felt like the rooms that Susan and I were in were inserted, if you would, into the outer shell of that structure. The interior did not match the exterior.

The P. I. put more salt on his scrambled eggs.

-If we get past tomorrow, I've gotta' pay that place a visit. And, another thing, Marlena, that black hole you spotted on the second floor-

-Yes?

-It matches what we saw at the seance. You didn't get too close to it, did you? Could be dangerous.

-No, but-

Marlena chose her words with care.

-But, there was something in it...floating to the surface.

-Like what?

-A body. It was a woman's body that had been horribly burned.

Edward put his strip of half eaten bacon back on to his plate.

-Did you recognize who it was? My sister disappeared through that same black hole. My God! It could have been her. Was she alive?

-I don't think so. I ran down to fetch Susan, but it was too late to do anything but flee for our lives.

-I'll call Lt. Donovan and have him send some men out there. It's a slim chance, but she might still be alive.

Marlena drank her coffee and didn't give voice to her next thought.

-They should leave her there to die. She's as good as dead.

Aloud.

-I'll call the Lieutenant, Edward. You need to rest. Why don't you go upstairs and I'll have Susan wake you in a few hours.

-I'm waiting on a call from the lieutenant. I should be up to get it.

-Which probably won't come for another few hours. Lange has to get his calculations ready and get a hold of his secretary; although why he needs her is beyond me. She struck me as being rather dull.

-I am kind of wiped out. Maybe, I will head on upstairs, but-

-Good boy. Now, get yourself into bed. Better yet, relax in a warm bath and have another cigarette. The heat is up so there should be enough hot water.

Edward finished his breakfast. Reluctantly, he climbed the carpeted stairs. Marlena had been right: people do give themselves away. She knew Holderman and his habits and his character. What else did she know about him?

-Plenty, I bet.

And, what else had Marlena said earlier in the day that had bothered him? Had it been said to Susan or Yolanda or even to himself? He couldn't recall it. He'd ask Yolanda, that is, after he'd finished taking a much needed bath.

Lt. Donovan's call came at 4 o'clock that afternoon. Susan took the call and relayed the message on to Edward who was now sitting, once again, in the small interview room.

-Professor Lange is on his way with his secretary. They had to stop at his office in midtown.

-Tomorrow will be the day? Is that definite?

Lt. Donovan took a sip of his black coffee.

-It's definite, all right. The time is set for 11 A.M. at the top of the Empire State Building. You know, I've never been there.

-Neither have I. But, why the change in venue?

-The professor said something about the curvature of the horizon favoring the midtown location. Did you know that they're thinking of placing a giant antennae on top of the 102nd story? It's to improve radio and eventually television reception.

-I hadn't heard that. Might look kinda' nice: pointing to infinity.

-Let's hope we live to see it. Anyway, we'll set up on the 86th floor observation deck and that will give us the four points of the compass to maneuver in. The building will be closed to the general public from this evening until-

-Until we're either successful or-

-No "either," Mendez. We either bring the sun back or this planet of ours will be a frozen ice cube in space.

Edward nodded in agreement and asked his next question.

-What's up with Holderman?

-He dodged our tail.

-I was afraid of that. He's cunning and he's got military training.

-Don't worry, the bastard won't get far: all the airports are shut down and all out of town trains have been cancelled. And, after tomorrow, I'll personally lead the manhunt for him. We'll get him.

-I wouldn't mind being in on that manhunt.

-You're welcome any time.

Edward took out a cigarette and lit up.

-Who'll be there tomorrow?

-You, me, Professor Lange and his secretary and a battalion of armed police officers.

-I'd like Yolanda to be there, too.

-Thought you might. Anyone else?

Edward laughed.

-I'm sure Miss Marlena Lake will insist on coming.

-I've met that bitch only once. You know, Mendez, we've got a file on her and her family.

-I'd be surprised if you didn't. How thick?

-The size of the King James Bible. We know that she and a group of her friends, which involves you, by the

way, took a plane ride to Germany a few months ago. Her son never came back from that trip. Would you happen to know why?

Edward had to take a deep drag on his cigarette. He chose his words with the utmost professional care; but, his answer was honest and direct.

-Mr. Gabriel Broder was killed and buried in Egypt.

Lt. Donovan leaned back in his chair

-That, we didn't know. Want to add a few more details to that statement?

-He was stabbed in self defense. His assailant was never found. The case in Egypt is still open.

-Go on.

Now, the P. I. had to lie.

-I don't know much else. The man who attacked him was thought to be a foreigner, possibly a terrorist.

-Not Egyptian?

-That's probably right.

-We'll contact the Cairo police about this when we've got the time.

Edward put out his cigarette.

-They might not be too cooperative. I didn't find them to be all that friendly; hostile might be a better word. They don't like anyone trampling on their toes.

-We'll still have to try. Gabriel Broder was an American citizen, so we owe him that much. Did Miss Lake contact the American embassy?

-No. She didn't. She doesn't trust authority in any country.

Lt. Donovan laughed out loud.

-And, *we* don't trust Miss Lake. Anyway, Mendez, bring her along tomorrow.

For just a moment, there was a silence between the two men. Edward lit another Lucky Strike while the Lieutenant played with his cup of coffee. The police detective broke that silence.

-Mendez? Miss Lake phoned us earlier about your sister, Catrina. She gave us some rather cryptic information about a house out in Staten Island that we might want to take a look at.

-Typical Marlena. But, did you find my sister out there?

-Yes. She was in the house or what was left of it. It was practically caving in on my men. We got your sister out just in the nick of time.

Edward was puzzled.

-Are you trying to tell me that my sister is alive? Marlena thought she was probably dead.

-I can understand Miss Lake thinking that. At first sight, Sgt. Rayno thought that she *was* dead, too. She's alive, Mendez, barely.

Lt. Donovan took a sip of his now cold coffee and looked Edward square in the eye.

-Dare I ask what your sister was doing in that part of town?

-I think I know how she got there, but who inflicted the injuries…I'd only be guessing.

-Let's start with how she got there?

Edward told him the details of the seance. The police detective put both hands to his head.

-Christ! Just a few days ago, I would've booked you into Bellevue for a story like that.

Edward smiled.

-And, now?

-Maybe, I oughta' book myself in.

-Where is Catrina now?

-They took her over to St. Vincent's They don't hold out much hope for her. She was burned real bad and…

-Go on. I'm thick skinned enough to hear it.

-She may have been blinded.

-My God! Have you notified my family?

-Not yet.

-Good. I'll do that. And, the prognosis?

-Not good. Looks to be radiation burns over most of her body.

Edward was in his downtown office with he feet propped up on his desk. He'd spoken to Nella. She would break the news to their sisters and mother about Catrina. How would his mother take the news? He had a strange feeling about that. Maybe the old woman had been expecting it or something like it for a long time.

The P. I. thought about the father whom he had never known. Who had given his father the spear or had he stolen it? And, that thought surprised Edward: to think of his own father as a thief.

Dottie had decided to take the subway home to Brooklyn instead of the elevated line. It had been an easy decision to make. The ride into Manhattan this morning hadn't been too bad until the train had to cross the Williamsburg Bridge. Dottie had made the mistake of looking down into the water…it was utter blackness and when she turned her gaze toward the the bridge, there was nothing to distinguish it from the blackness below. Was the train suspended in mid-air? Common sense told her that this was impossible…so she closed her eyes until the train entered the subway tunnel in Manhattan.

Now, she was safely tucked away on the LL underground line heading back home. The subway car was well lit and one could at least pretend that things above ground were as they used to be. The train had just pulled out of the Graham Avenue station and nobody had gotten on or off. Still, there were a few passengers keeping her company. Dottie even nodded to a few of them. She wasn't one to stand on ceremony or formality. The heater under her seat wasn't working, but she was well bundled up in her coat, woolen scarf and hat.

She had just put down her newspaper on the seat next to her; there were some wild rumors of people in California making for the Carlsbad Caverns to take underground shelter. What was the point? So they could starve to death or freeze more slowly into a popsicle? Dottie let out a good laugh and was tempted to pick up the paper, again. Instead, she looked about at some of the advertisements on the top portion of the car: Chesterfield cigarettes, Perfume deParis, and there was a photo of the latest Miss Subways. Dottie grinned at seeing that last one.

-Where did they dig her up from? My sister, Victoria, oughta' be there.

And…was that Angel sitting in the far corner? Yes. It was. And, he was sitting with a very pretty girl with short red hair. The girl was wearing pants and boots to match and she had a cavalier way about her.

-The Bohemian type, I'll bet.

The two of them were talking intently, but Dottie had no way of overhearing them and that was good. If she had heard their conversation, she might have fled into the next car or even gotten off the train.

It was just past 3 P.M. when Dottie got off the train and headed upstairs to the exit. Angel and his girlfriend had not gotten off and she wondered about that.

-Angel must have left the gym and met up with his girlfriend. Didn't know he had one.

Outside, it was darker than it had been underground. Dottie Mendez walked as fast as she could to get out of the darkness and the cold and that wretched wind that never let up. She was thinking of how it had been a not-so-lousy day at the office: at least half the staff hadn't showed up for work and the insurance policies were not coming in. Who the hell needed insurance anymore? Who would be around to collect on it? The workers had been let out early: the "non-essential" personnel as her so-called superiors had put it. Good. Now her darling manager, who had made life so miserable, was stuck in a cold office by herself.

Smiling, she was about to turn the corner on Linden St. and Knickerbocker Ave. when she felt eyes staring at her. The lamp post was giving off light, but the darkness right beyond it was pitch black. Dottie stopped walking and stayed under the imagined safety of the lamp post, but how long could she just stand there? Someone was watching her. Was it from above? She looked up and saw a shooting star; hardly the stuff of nightmares. She turned to her left and, then, to her right, nothing but blackness with the occasional lamp posts throwing off circles of light.

Dottie was standing in front of a candy store. She looked into the glass window and almost laughed out loud with relief. It was Stripes, the tabby cat, who was watching her. She decided to go in and pay the old couple who owned the store a visit.

-Hello? Anybody here?

Dottie went over to the cat and picked him up. He was friendly and cuddly and she was quite in love with the little guy. The shopkeeper, an elderly woman, emerged from the back room.

-Oh, hello, Dottie. It's so good to see someone. Business has been terrible and the streets seem so deserted. I've been so afraid.

-Honey, you can say that, again! I'll take my usual assortment of licorice if you have any. I'm officially off my latest diet.

-I'll get if for you.

The old lady went to get a brown paper bag and scooper. She looked over her shoulder at her customer.

-You really like Stripes, don't you? He likes you.

-Love him.

-We can't keep him.

Dottie looked up from her little game with the cat.

-Why? Is something wrong. Is Jack not feeling well?

-He's fine; but, we're going to be moving into an old age residence. We can keep some of our own furniture, but they don't allow pets.

-What will you do with this little guy? You're not just going to put him out, are you?

-We don't want to. I-

-What is is, honey?

Dottie could see that the old lady was close to tears.

-Would you take him, Dottie? I know you love him and he sure loves you. Do you think you might?

Dottie was on the verge of tears herself.

-You bet I will! I'm going to be moving back home in a couple of weeks; that is, if we have a couple of weeks left! I'll take real good care of him. When are you and Jack leaving?

-The first of the year. That is, like you say, if there is a first of the year.

Dottie stroked the tabby under his chin.

-Just give me a day or two to get things ready for him. And, if there is a God, there will be a tomorrow.

And, with that Dottie burst into tears.

PART V

THE GREEN TORCH
December 17, 1947

CHAPTER TWENTY-ONE

EDWARD, YOLANDA, Susan, and Marlena were picked up by a squad car the next morning in front of Marlena's townhouse. The gale force wind that had hit the northeastern coast had not let up and now it threatened to snow again. It was past the morning rush hour, or what was left of that rush hour, and traffic was light. Lt. Donovan and a police officer sat in the front seat with Edward. The ladies were in the back seat much to Marlena'a annoyance.

-I wish I could say it was a nice morning, but those mornings have been put on hold lately. Maybe permanently.

Lt. Donovan looked straight ahead without looking at anyone in the car. The expression on his face wasn't a pleasant one.

-No response? Mendez? Miss Lake?

-What would you have us say, Lieutenant? Perhaps, tomorrow there will be a sunrise with many more to come.

-Do you really think so, Miss Lake? You don't strike me as being the optimistic type.

-Why the sarcasm? Get up on the wrong side of the bed?

-Mother…don't. We've no time for this. Not now.

-As a matter of fact, Miss Lake, I didn't get any sleep at all last night.

-Where is the spear?

Marlena waited for an answer from Lt. Donovan. His silence spoke volumes even to Marlena. She didn't press the issue.

The patrol car drove past 34th St. and continued downtown. It started snowing, but not too heavily.

Edward spoke up and even looked at Lt. Donovan.

-Hey, we missed our turn off. What gives?

-Did we, Mendez?

-Okay, Donovan, I give up. What the hell is going on?

-He hasn't answered my question, Edward. Where is the spear, cop? I demand to know.

Still staring straight ahead, this time, he answered her.

-Safe on board the ferry. And, just watch that mouth of yours, lady.

-What are you saying? Edward told us that the Empire State Building had been decided upon.

Lt. Donovan smiled.

-That's right, sister. But, it was decided yesterday that the Statue of Liberty would be the best and safest vantage point to fire off the spear.

-And, just who the hell decided that? Was it Professor Lange?

Susan interjected.

-Mother, there's no point in arguing with what's already been decided. Lt. Donovan obviously doesn't trust us.

Edward turned to face the Lieutenant.

-You were holding out on me. Susan is right: you don't trust us. That's it, isn't it? I thought you were on the level with me, pal. I'm real sorry about that.

-The fewer who knew about it, the better. We did it for your own good.

Edward lost his temper.

-You're full of crap, pal. I'm the one who can operate that little spear. I should have known. I had a *right* to know, damn it! My sister, Nella, once told me as a little boy to put your trust in only two things: myself and God; and, brother, was she right.

Yolanda sat forward and tapped the Lt. Donovan on the shoulder, much to that man's annoyance..

-And, maybe we don't trust you either? Have you ever thought of that? Why should we?

-That's your privilege.

Yolanda touched Edward on the shoulder.

-Edward, didn't I tell you that we should have taken the spear to Marlena's with us last night? This cop is nothing but a liar and a thief.

-Next time, I'll listen, baby. You can count on it.

An uneasy silence permeated the cold air in the patrol car. No one spoke to each other or even looked at each other with the exception of Yolanda. She stared at the Lieutenant with loathing and contempt in her eyes. Marlena sat there in silence, plotting her next move which was taking possession of the spear because in her mind, it was *her* spear.

No one saw the black armored car until it was almost on top of them. It tried cutting off the patrol car at 14th St. just at the cross section that separated midtown Manhattan from the Westside Village. The armored car tried ramming them as the squad car emerged on to 14th St. The officer driving floored the gas pedal and narrowly avoided getting blindsided. Accelerating now at close to 90 mph, the squad car was only a few feet ahead of its pursuer who had cut them off from their police escort.

Lt. Donovan shouted at the driver.

-Open her up, officer. We've got to make it to that ferry. Move it!

The driver gunned the motor.

Edward took out his gun and cracked open the car window. Yolanda saw what he was about to do.

-Edward, be careful! They could have a gunman in that car, too.

Marlena gave her pointed advice.

-And, don't waste a shot. Go for the front tires.

The P. I. leaned out the window, took aim and fired. He hit the right front tire, but nothing happened. He fired a second shot and hit the same tire and this time, a popping sound followed by a loud hiss could be heard. The armored car started swerving from left to right. It side swiped a couple of parked cars, narrowly missed a couple of pedestrians, hit a lamppost and flipped over on its side crashing into a storefront. The driver and his two hitmen tried getting out of the van as it caught fire and exploded, burning them alive.

-Nice shooting, Mendez.

Edward didn't answer. He was still furious with him. He put his gun back in his shoulder holster and sat back.

The squad car reached the ferry terminal and they were greeted by a small battalion of police officers. They were escorted on to the boat. Within a few minutes, the ferry was under way, but not before another earth tremor hit and this one caused an upheaval in the bay. Everyone on board held their breath until the tremor subsided.

As the planet tremor ended, the former occupants of the squad car paired off. Edward and Marlena went with Lt. Donovan to check on the spear and plan their strategy. Professor Lange and his secretary, Mary, were waiting for them inside the ship's cabin.

Yolanda and Susan stayed outside on deck. They were holding on to the ship's railing and looking out at the water which was anything but a reassuring sight: white caps foaming everywhere, waves hitting the ships hull, and the now constant wind along with the falling snow.

-Well, Susan, what do you think of our Lt. Donovan? I think I despise him. He lied to my boyfriend.

-I can see the contempt in his eyes when he looks at any one of us. Sorry. But, I'm still catching my breath from that last tremor.

Both women took a few more moments to compose themselves.

-I noticed that hard look, too. And, he doesn't try to hide it, either. He wouldn't make a very good diplomat.

-He questioned you about Dolores the other day, didn't he? That must have been awkward. What on earth did you tell him? What *could* you tell him? Not the truth.

-It was awkward, all right. He didn't believe anything that I told him. Too bad.

-Did he actually know Dolores?

-I doubt it. She never mentioned him to me, and she told me everything.

-What was my mother's attitude toward Lt. Donovan?

-She was busy antagonizing him.

-That doesn't surprise me.

-Come to think of it, she didn't really seem worried. She was more annoyed than actually worried or concerned.

-Now, that's interesting. But, how was Dolores' body identified?

-Through her I. D.

-What kind of I. D. would hold up under water for so long?

-That's what Edward wanted to know. I don't know. Lt. Donovan didn't say.

-How could my brother, Gabriel, have been so careless? That wasn't like him at all.

That's not what Susan had wanted to say. She knew that her mother was a long range planner. If Gabriel had been careless enough to leave identification on Dolores' corpse, it had been done so under orders: her mother's orders. And, another thought hit Susan which she kept to herself: had her mother tipped off the police? It was a distinct possibility and a very clever way of keeping Edward and Yolanda under her control.

Yolanda looked up at the Milky Way.

-Dolores wanted to leave your mother's group. I can tell you that now. She wasn't happy with her life.

-I suspected as much. I know she didn't trust my mother.

-Did your mother suspect that Dolores wanted to leave?

-My mother is sharp. If I suspected then so did she. Nothing gets by her radar.

Both women laughed.

-I wonder…

-What are you thinking, Susan?

-I wonder if the Lieutenant *did* know Dolores and was in love with her. It's rather romantic, if you stop to think about it.

-Then, maybe it's time he got over it.

-He may not want to.

The rough waters of the bay were rocking the boat. It started to snow more heavily.

-Susan? What is it?

-I was thinking about that Lodge house.

-What about it?

-The police said it was caving in and that makes no sense, Yolanda. The structure was sound enough.

-Edward wants to pay that place a visit. He's pretty curious about it.

-So am I. You should have seen the incredible library in there. I hope we can salvage a few books.

Inside the ship's cabin, the spear had been placed atop one of the benches. It was in a lead lined box with two police officers guarding it. Professor Lange was standing closest to it and fending off Marlena.

-I insist on seeing it.

-No, Miss Lake. For your own safety, be patient. As I was saying ... once outside on the arm of the statue, I can easily calculate where the sun should be. You will aim the spear, Mr. Mendez, directly at the sun's core and that should bring it back.

-How long do I hold it in place, Professor?

-Until the sun reappears. The color spectrum may change and be distracting. You will hold the spear steady until our star regains its original color which is actually white and not yellow.

Lt. Donovan picked up the conversation.

-My men will form a phalanx around the statue's base. I'll also send men up to the crown and station a few others outside the arm to form a bodyguard. They'll be armed with sub-machine guns and hand grenades per Mendez's instructions.

-If any black hole appears, Lieutenant, toss everything you've got into it and don't miss.

-Don't worry, Mendez, I've got the best marksmen on the force with us.

-So, it'll be me and the professor out on the torch.

-No!

-Miss Lake?

-I'll be there, as well, and don't even think of trying to stop me.

Lt. Donovan stared hard at Marlena.

-I wouldn't dream of stopping you.

-And, where will *you* be, Lieutenant?

-Right behind *you*, lady.

CHAPTER TWENTY-TWO

THE WATER was even rougher and more turbulent than it had been just twenty minutes ago when the boat left the South Ferry Terminal. It took four unsuccessful attempts before they could maneuver the boat in.

Two police officers carried the spear off of the boat and into the statue's base. Four officers went ahead and four others followed. Professor Lange, Edward, Marlena, and Lt. Donovan followed these four cops into the base of the pedestal. Mary Riley stayed just outside the entrance with the other police officers in spite of the brutal wind and snow.

Once inside the base, Lt. Donovan directed them toward the two elevators that would carry them up to the actual foot of the statue.

Yolanda and Susan caught up to them.

-Edward, I'm going with you.

-It's gonna' be dangerous up there, baby.

-I don't care about that. I just want to be with you.

Lt. Donovan addressed the figure skater.

-You and Miss Broder will have to wait it out at the base of the arm. The structure of the arm will support only so many people, Miss Estravades.

-Then, I'll be waiting on the spiral staircase and so will Susan. We won't be far away.

Everyone entered the two elevators. The doors closed and they were on their way up to the statue. The other Police Officers had already started climbing the many stairwells. The sound of heavy footsteps reverberated in the statue's base but few words were exchanged.

The occupants in the elevator car stared straight ahead. Yolanda held on to Edward's arm and wanted to say something to her boyfriend, but what? What could she say? that she loved him? Yes.

Marlena cast an occasional furtive glance at the crate that held the spear. She was still upset with Edward for not bringing it to her place the other night. What secrets did that ancient weapon possess? She had to know.

The elevator came to a halt and the doors slid open. The occupants moved toward the spiral staircase that led up the the crown and the torch. It was a narrow and steep circular staircase. Lt. Donovan led the way up and the two officers carrying the spear followed close behind with Edward following them. Marlena, Susan, Yolanda, and the other police officers brought up the rear.

After a twenty minute climb, Edward, Professor Lange, and Marlena veered off to the spiral staircase leading into the statue's arm and upward to the torch.

Lt. Donovan ordered the two officers with the spear to proceed. upward. He, then, issued orders for some officers to head on up to the statue's crown. A few officers were stationed on the balcony of the statue. All the police officers were heavily armed. Lt. Donovan also had two men stay with Yolanda and Susan for protection.

The two police officers came out on to the torch. It was still snowing and the wind was kicking up, blowing the crystalline snow about. And, the arm moved…it was the stress factor that had been built into the statue to prevent in from snapping off in the harbor's extreme weather. The two cops exchanged looks. They had expected the movement because they'd been warned about it, but it was still pretty unnerving.

Edward and Marlena stepped out on to the narrow, circular balcony. The black sky was ablaze with shooting meteorites. And, the Manhattan skyline was equally impressive with every window in every skyscraper lit. It was a jeweled canvas against the purity of the heavens.

The two police officers set the crate down and went back into the torch to guard the entrance. Lt. Donovan stepped out with Professor Lange right behind him. As the professor emerged, his hat was blown off by the wind.

-I just bought that last week.

-We'll get you a new one, Professor.

-Thank you, Lieutenant.

Edward squatted down next to the crate. Marlena handed him his protective gloves and whispered in his ear.

-Be careful, Edward. Don't hold on to the spear any longer than you must.

The P. I. flipped open the box's lid and took out the spear. He straightened up holding on to it. The metal tip was radiating a dark, green light. The blade was rectangular, but shaped more like a geometric trapezoid.

Professor Lange came over.

-Edward, move a few paces to your left. Stop. In a few minutes, it will be time to begin. We must try and aim for the sun's core.

-I'm ready right now, Professor. This *will* work.

-Was that a question or a statement?

-A little of both.

-So is my answer, Mr. Mendez. Now, point the spear at this angle.

As Professor Lange showed Edward where to point the weapon, Marlena and Lt. Donovan noticed a speck of black appear in mid-air. It was several yards away from them, but it was widening in diameter.

Marlena shouted out.

-Look! They're going to try and stop us. Lieutenant, take aim at it and don't miss.

Lt. Donovan had already drawn his gun and aimed at the black disc hovering in the sky. He fired straight into it. The two police officers standing guard came out and aimed their sub-machine guns at the disc. The black disc kept expanding...getting closer to the torch.

Lt. Donovan shouted out his orders.

-Toss your hand grenades into it!

The two officers reached back into the entrance way for the crate of grenades. In the meantime, the officers stationed in the crown were breaking every window. They were getting ready to fire into the black disc. The police on the ground were aiming their guns skyward at it.

Marlena leaned over the railing.

-Careful, Miss Lake.

-Lieutenant, throw those hand grenades in *now*. That black disc mustn't touch this statue.

Lt. Donovan gave the order. He and his two men starting throwing in hand grenades. They exploded inside the disc and bizarre noises could be heard…debase noises.

Marlena shouted to no one in particular.

-It's working. What you're hearing are those androids being destroyed. Keep tossing those grenades in.

They did. And, the men stationed in the statue's crown trained their guns on the enemy target. The black disc began to quiver. It tilted in a way that the people on the statue could see into its depths. Blue images of humanoid forms were trying to crawl out of it. The officers' machine gun fire knocked the humanoids back into the black disc. More hand grenades were tossed into it from the statue's arm and now the disc was breaking up into fragments that started to disintegrate.

The people on the torch stared into the now peaceful darkness. The snow kept coming down and the wind was still kicking up, but the air was filled with a momentary victory.

Lt. Donovan focused his attention back to their objective.

-Okay, Professor, you just about ready? Mendez?

The P. I. was about to answer when he was forced to stop short. Professor Lange was pointing a gun straight at him. Edward stared at Professor Lange straight in the eye.

-What are you up to, pal? You signaled to your cronies before, didn't you? The old hat-blown-off trick. Rotten, stinking bastard!

-Careful, Mr. Mendez or I will blow your head off. Now, hand me the spear like a good boy.

-Forget it. Donovan? Get this creep. Never mind about me.

Lt. Donovan addressed Professor Lange.

-Professor Lange, step away from Mendez. We've only a couple of minutes left. Do you want us all to freeze to death? Don't be a fucking idiot.

-I am no idiot. I will take the spear and you will make certain of my escape, Lt.

-Forget it. Mendez? Hold on to that spear.

Marlena opened her pocketbook and placed her hand on her gun. She spoke to the Professor.

-Professor Lange, why are you doing this foolish thing? You can't possibly get away. I never thought of you as a stupid man.

-Miss Lake, I plan to join my comrades. The world will freeze over; but we will survive in hiding. It'll be a pleasure knowing that you're dead, lady.

-We'll just see about that.

Marlena drew her gun and fired. She was a crack shot and at this distance, half of Professor Lange's head was blown off. Edward swung the spear and pushed the dead man over the rail. The body plummeted to the ground. Down below, a woman's scream could be heard.

Lt. Donovan shouted at Marlena.

-Are you crazy? Only he knew where to point that damned thing.

-He'd never have told us. Get my daughter, Susan, up here; and be quick about it. She knows where to point the spear. *Hurry!*

Lt. Donovan ran past the two officers and down the spiral stairs like a madman.

-Susan! We need you up on the torch. Come on!

Susan didn't hesitate. Her mother had warned her to be ready for either the Empire State Building or the Statue of Liberty. Marlena didn't trust anyone, least of all the fuzz. She followed Lt Donovan and Yolanda, in turn, followed her up the spiral stairwell.

In a matter of minutes, they were all crowded on to the exterior of the torch. Susan, holding on to the railing for balance, went over to Edward.

-Edward, point the spear directly overhead. I'll help you position it.

The P. I. crouched down on one knee and pointed the spear skyward. Susan took out a collapsible telescope from her shoulder bag and a sextant.

-To the left...just a little...stop! It should be pointing at the sun's core. Mother, what time is it? I need a precise time.

-11:30.

Susan took a deep breath.

-Now, Edward. It has to be now! Focus your mind. Focus your intent.

The P. I. gripped the spear and spoke.

-Let it be...*now*!

A blinding green ray of light shot out from the spear. Everyone, except the P. I. turned away from the glare. The ray reached up through the atmosphere at the speed of light...and it hit its target: the sun's core. For a moment, there was utter blackness except for the spear's light and, then, the blackness shimmered and the darkness gave way to a pinpoint of white light which expanded into a giant sphere which men call the sun.

The spear's green ray shot back into the weapon. Edward dropped it to the ground. Yolanda, pushing past Lt. Donovan, helped Edward to stand up. He staggered forward and had to hold on to the railing of the torch for support.

It was daylight once more and the sun shone brilliant in the blue sky. Susan and Lt. Donovan hugged each other. The police officers cheered and so did everyone else in that great city.

Marlena bent down to pick up the spear, but it was nowhere to be found. It had done its work.

-Where is it? I must have it.

Susan went over to her distraught mother.

-My mother. Forget about that spear. The world's been saved, for heaven's sake.

Marlena was not consoled.

At the other end of the balcony, Yolanda stroked Edward's face.

-Edward, are you all right? What's wrong, my love?

-Yolanda…I can't see. I'm blind.

-Oh, my God! What are you saying? Try to blink your eyes a few times.

Edward tried blinking.

-It's like a green haze. I can't see beyond it.

Marlena overheard this and forgot about the spear.

-Edward? It's Marlena. I'm sure it's only temporary. Try and stay calm, dear boy.

Susan, who was standing next to Edward, touched his arm.

-It's probably like being blinded by a camera's flash. I'm sure it will fade. Lt. Donovan? We need to get Edward to a hospital.

-Mendez? We'll take you over to Bellevue. Can you walk?

Yolanda was angry.

-Of course he can walk. He's blinded not crippled. Edward? Edward?

-I'm here, baby. Just help me down.

-We'll take good care of you, Mendez. I'll go on ahead and alert the medics.

The five people left the torch and made their way down the spiral staircase.

EPILOGUE

HOLDERMAN WAS a desperate man. Desperate for escape. He knew the cops had a tail on him. What of it? He'd outwitted them.

Wulf Holderman walked the streets brooding and planning what to do next. He was cold, but not tired from his walk around Central Park and most of the upper east side of Manhattan. His military training gave him enough stamina to keep going and to hide out from any squad car that might come cruising by. Had Marshal Law been declared? He wasn't sure. He didn't care.

It was just past 9:30 A.M. when he spotted the squad cars driving down 2nd Avenue. He hid in the recess of a storefront. Yes. He saw the P. I. and Lt. Donovan in the front seat.

-My God, they must have the spear with them. Can they save this damned world or will they end up destroying it?

Holderman watched them drive by before he emerged from hiding and, then, continued on his way downtown. The snow was coming down heavier. It stung his eyes and made walking that much more difficult. The constant wind didn't help either. He'd stopped cursing the weather several hours ago. What was the point?

He walked into a barber shop on Lexington Ave near Grand Central Station. He needed a haircut and he needed to get out of the damned cold. There was one other patron already on the barber's chair: a young boy of no more than eighteen. He looked frightened, but not at anything in particular. Perhaps, the world's destruction had affected him. Holderman felt sorry for the boy. Like himself, he was probably a loner with few friends. And, yes, he had caught sight of Holderman in the mirror. They exchanged looks and nodded to each other: a gesture that was difficult for the both of them. The boy got off the barber's chair and paid up. Unlike Holderman, he didn't have much money on him: just enough to cover the haircut and a modest T.I.P.

The barber beckoned Holderman to take the chair. The ex-Nazi got up and walked the few feet to the chair. He addressed the boy.

-Don't look so worried. We may all die together, but we may all end up living. Keep your head up and look me in the eye. That's right. Nice haircut, you got; keep it that short length.

-Thanks. I'd better get home. I wanted to visit Manhattan one last time.

-It may not be the last time. Be strong and think only of yourself. Remember what I tell you.

-I will.

-Practice what I tell you.

-So long.

Holderman ordered the barber not to cut his blonde hair too short because he wanted to fit in with the crowds of people in the street. The barber did a decent job and was given a minimum T.I.P.

Now, for some food. He checked his wallet: it was stuffed with a wad of bills. Holderman stopped off at the automat just a couple of blocks away from the barber shop and selected a grilled ham and cheese sandwich and some coffee. Not bad; but, he wouldn't go out of his way to come back. The place was clean enough, but did not stand up to his strict German standards.

He bit into his sandwich and barely tasted what he ate.

Fools. The word reverberated in his head. His so-called comrades had made it down to Antarctica before the war had ended and found the ruins of an ancient civilization: a city that lay half buried and frozen in that God forsaken wasteland. They'd managed to salvage some of the technology but they had not mastered it by any means. The plan: project the sun into a parallel universe and freeze the planet. Having committed this mass genocide, they'd bring the sun back into its proper dimension and establish the Fourth Reich. But, they would need the Spear of Longinus to do it. The spear was, in fact, part of the lost technology that had long ago vanished from the city. They had deciphered the ancient records and knew this.

The impatient fools! They should have waited until they actually had the damned spear once again in their possession. They knew that Manuel Mendez had known how to use it: that supreme egotist whom they all hated. The old man and his stupid wife who had thought herself superior to everyone. Mrs. Mendez had learned her lesson the hard way: don't venture forth where no one wants you.

The spear had been taken from Mendez's crypt. Holderman had done that himself and had delivered it to his Chancellor. Hoffman, Sr. had been lied to as well as the Frenchwoman and both of them had been led to believe that the spear had been lost upon Mendez's death. The Party didn't trust either one of those characters, but they could serve a future use.

Fate, as it usually does, had played its cruel trick. Hitler had lost possession of the spear and, once again, Hoffman and the Frenchwoman had to be trusted with the task of finding it; but this time the hunt would be for real. Werner Hoffman, Jr. was sent to contact the son, Edward Mendez, to track it down; but, the boy had become too unreliable and had to be eliminated. Holderman had seen to that.

And, now Mendez and his friends had the artifact and even the cops were in on it. Would they succeed? Holderman had the feeling that they might.

Now what? Yes. Clothes. He needed a modest business suit that wouldn't attract attention. He found a haberdashers on Lexington Ave. and went in. His was an easy size to fit and he had no trouble getting into a dark grey suit. The owner was grateful because business had been bad lately.

Holderman tried on a Fedora hat. And, then…the sun came out in one blinding instant. He and the owner looked out the shop's window. People were running out on to the sidewalks and yelling with unrestrained joy. He joined them and found himself standing next to an unusual looking young man with wire rimmed spectacles. The young man wore a bomber jacket and ski cap. He moved closer to Holderman…a little too close.

-Sun's out. It's beautiful.

-Yes. I can see that.

-You're German. I'm Spanish.

-Oh? Should that interest me?

-My name is Angel Correa.

-Should I know you?

-No. I'm just walking downtown. What about you?

-Your accent is strange, Mr. Correa.

-Angel. Well, heading my way downtown? I'm not going that far.

-Yes. As a matter of fact, I am.

The two men walked toward 18th St. passing among the many rejoicing people. They didn't speak to each other.

-Well, young man, I am at my destination. Good day.

-May I come in?

Holderman hesitated. He got out the key to open the shop's door and noticed that his hand was trembling.

-I've much to do. And, I won't be staying long.

-I won't stay long. Please. I need to use your bathroom or else I wouldn't ask.

-Very well.

The two men entered the book shop, but only one man walked out alive.

COMING SOON

THE IMMORTAL
An Edward Mendez, P. I. Thriller
Book III

by
Gerard Denza

ABOUT THE AUTHOR

Gerard Denza has worked in the Publicity Dept. at Random House and Little, Brown, and Co. in New York City. He's worked with such authors as Pete Hamill, Arthur C. Clarke, Willie Morris, Pat Booth, and Kevin and Todd Berger. He's the author and director of six Off-Off Broadway plays that include:

ICARUS, MAHLER: THE MAN WHO WAS NEVER BORN, THE DYING GOD: A VAMPIRE'S TALE, SHADOWS BEHIND THE FOOTLIGHTS, and THE HOUSEDRESS. His noir play, EDMUND: THE LIKELY, has been recorded for radio broadcast.

Mr. Denza is a graduate of Fordham University at Lincoln Center where he majored in psychology. He is also the author of ICARUS: THE COLLECTED PLAYS, THE TIME DECEIVER: AN EDWARD MENDEZ, P. I. THRILLER and RAMSAY: DEALER OF DEATH.

He can be contacted at www.gerarddenza.com.

He lives in New York City and is hard at work on his next novel: THE IMMORTAL: AN EDWARD MENDEZ, P. I. THRILLER, BOOK III.